The Ghosts of Aquinnah

By Julie Flanders

Ink Smith Publishing

www.ink-smith.com

ISBN: 978-1-939156-20-4

Ink Smith Publishing

P.O Box 1086

Glendora CA

For my mom, who taught me at a young age about the magic to be found within the pages of a book. And for my grandfather, who gave me the treasure that is Martha's Vineyard, and my grandmother, whose Irish blood runs deep in my veins.

January 18, 1884

The trip had started out so well.

Christopher Casey had jumped at the chance to move to Savannah, Georgia and leave Boston behind. The brutal New England winter chilled him to his bones and left him longing for his home across the sea in Galway. When he'd heard of the opportunities to work on the Savannah docks loading cotton he hadn't thought twice about heading south.

He'd saved his wages and sold his few belongings and finally raised the $15 he needed to buy a steerage ticket on *The City of Columbus*. That morning, he'd been so excited about the upcoming trip he'd almost forgotten about the cold and fever that had been plaguing him for days.

"You should wait for another boat, Christopher," his landlady Mrs. Pitts had insisted as she poured him a cup of hot coffee. "You're not well enough to make that trip."

"Nonsense. I'll be right as rain as soon as I'm out to sea, sailing under the sunshine…"

An ill-timed coughing fit had interrupted his declaration.

"Now doesn't that prove what I'm trying to tell you," Mrs. Pitts said. "Listen to yourself, lad. You'll end up with the consumption long before you ever make it to Georgia."

Christopher gulped down his coffee and stood up from his landlady's table. "Don't be daft. I'm not going to get the consumption." He took Mrs. Pitts' hand in his own and lightly kissed it with his lips. "I do appreciate your concern though, Mrs. Pitts. And I can't deny I'm going to miss you. And your coffee."

The portly woman laughed and momentarily looked 20 years younger than her true age of 50 as her cheeks turned a flaming shade of crimson. "You'll miss the coffee most of all, I'm sure of that."

"You're surely wrong then."

"I can't convince you to wait? They'll be plenty of other voyages going south. Come back here tonight and let me take care of you. Get ya well before you head on out to sea."

Christopher shook his head. "No, I'm going now. If I let something like a little catarrh stop me I'll never get anywhere."

He'd left Mrs. Pitts' boarding house for his last day's work on the Boston docks, then bounded aboard *The City of Columbus* with a few dollars in his pocket and a spring in his step. When the steamer had departed Boston under a cloudless winter sky he'd dreamed of the southern sunshine he'd heard so much about and started counting the hours until he'd feel warm again.

He now realized he hadn't even known what cold was then. But as his ice-encrusted fingers clutched the shrouds that had connected the steamer's masthead to the sides of the vessel, he knew.

Christopher had been sleeping in his bunk when he'd heard a loud crunching noise and felt the ship start to list. He'd jumped out of bed and pulled on his boots and grabbed his coat as the room tilted to one side and the floor seemed to slide under his feet. He'd struggled to keep his balance as he'd left the room and stumbled into the hallway, where he'd been greeted by a rush of water that reached his knees.

As the gushing water rose to his waist, Christopher cursed himself as he dropped his coat and watched as it was instantly carried away from him down the corridor. He ignored the cacophony of terrified screaming around him and made his way for the stairway he knew would lead him to the ship's deck. What he'd found there had been more horrifying than anything he ever could have imagined.

Instead of the safe harbor he'd hoped for, the deck had been nothing but terror and chaos. The ship's crew members haphazardly attempted to cut lifeboats free from their moorings, only to have the boats crash against the hull of the sinking ship and fall into the churning sea. Christopher had watched women clutching their children and men grabbing for lifejackets just as a huge wave engulfed the deck. When the wave receded, everyone and everything in its path had disappeared into the sea.

The starboard side of the ship was high in the air and Christopher had grasped the railing next to him with a strength he'd never known he had. Within minutes, the ship had started to right itself, and Christopher knew he had only seconds to get to safety before she sank. Having nowhere else to go, he'd leapt into the ship's rigging and climbed above the rising sea as the rest of *The City of Columbus* disappeared beneath him.

That had been hours ago. The screams and cries surrounding him had lessened with each passing hour, as one survivor after another fell into the sea. Christopher was no longer shivering as the wind rocked the mast he clung to and the blowing waves rose and drenched him with frigid water. He simply felt tired and too weak to continue holding on to the shrouds that had saved his life. His thick brown hair had turned to ice on his head, his clothing was frozen to his feverish body, and his hands and arms throbbed with pain.

But now he watched the sun rise on the opposite side of the island, punctuating the black sky around him with fiery stripes of red and orange. And Christopher realized that he wanted to keep trying. He could now clearly see the rocky shore less than a mile from him, and the keeper's house next to the red

3

brick lighthouse whose shining beacon had been his only source of hope throughout the pitch dark night. He'd watched the lighthouse and forced himself to count in rhythm along with the flashing lights, an endless cycle of three whites and one red.

Now, the site of the keeper's house gave Christopher more hope than the lights ever could. There were people in that house, and probably a town beyond it. And now that the morning had come, help would be coming too. Christopher was sure of it.

When he saw the boat rowing towards him through the waves, he wondered if he was simply hallucinating. But when he heard the men on the boat yell out for survivors, he knew they were real. And he knew that they were coming for him.

"Help!" he cried out, his voice croaking. "Over here, help us, please!"

Knowing he could not be heard above the noise of the wind and the surf, Christopher screamed louder. "Help!"

His anguished yells gave way to a fierce coughing fit that wracked his body and nearly caused Christopher to lose his hold on the rigging. As the boat moved closer, he could make out the thick coats and heavy life vests that the men aboard it wore and he knew he wouldn't have to hold on much longer. The man at the front of the boat raised an arm and waved to him.

"We see you!" he yelled.

Christopher burst into tears that immediately froze to ice on his pale face. "Help me, please," he said between violent coughs. "Please!"

"We can't get to you, boy," the man yelled. "We'll sink."

As Christopher looked down at the currents swirling around the submerged deck of the wrecked ship, he understood why his rescuers could not risk coming into the churning waters. The waves could easily grab their own boat and destroy it within seconds.

"Come to us!" The man held up a boathook. "We'll get you!"

Christopher knew there was nothing to do but let go and fall into the sea. He couldn't hold on any longer anyway. He stared at the men in the boat and then looked back down at the water. He pried his frozen fingers from the rigging and dropped into the waves below.

The icy water hit Christopher with the force of a train as the waves sucked him into the ocean. Using his last ounce of strength, he struggled to swim back to the surface. When his head came back above water he opened his mouth to yell to his rescuers just as a wave picked him up and sent him careening into the boat. As the water slammed Christopher into the side of the rescue boat, he felt a sharp pain in his left arm just before he lost consciousness.

When he came to he was on his back in the boat, stretched out next to the rowing men. He could see another survivor near the front of the boat but didn't have the strength to sit up and look for others. He noticed he was wrapped in a large blue coat and realized that one of the rescuers had removed their own coat and given it to him. The man glanced down at him now and nodded.

Christopher wanted to speak, to say thank you, but he was unable to say the words. Each time he opened his mouth, his lungs erupted into coughing fits that merely amplified the blinding pain in his arm. He shivered both from the frigid temperature and icy waters and from the fever that now raged through his body. Christopher's vision blurred and the sky above him slipped from view as he slipped mercifully back into unconsciousness.

May, 2013

Hannah Forrester stared out the window of her Boston apartment and watched the rain drench the street below her. It had been raining steadily for two days now, but it felt more like two hundred. The April showers had extended well into May, and she'd had enough rain to last a lifetime. She couldn't wait for the summer sunshine.

Hannah smoothed her long brown curly hair with her hands and tied it into a loose bun at the nape of her neck. She had tied and untied her hair at least five times since she'd sat down to work. She had also tied and untied the drawstring on her dark green pajama bottoms, and fastened and unfastened the buttons at the top of her cream-colored Henley shirt. In short, she had done everything besides what she was supposed to be doing, which was researching her book on New England lighthouses. She glanced down at her laptop and her legal pad full of scribbled notes and immediately focused her attention back on the rain.

"Is there a lighthouse out there I haven't noticed?"

Hannah jumped at the sound of the voice behind her. She turned and saw her boyfriend Jon Rodriguez walking into the room.

"I didn't even hear you come in," she said.

"I'm not surprised. You're too engrossed in the rain." He leaned down and kissed the top of Hannah's head.

"I thought you had surgery this evening."

"I did. It's finished." Jon sat down on their king-sized bed and started to remove his shoes. "It's 10:00, Hannah."

Hannah stretched and leaned back in her desk chair, massaging her shoulders with her hands. "I didn't realize it was that late. Time got away from me tonight."

"Tonight and just about every night lately. Are you getting anywhere on that book?"

"Not really."

Jon rolled his eyes. "I don't know why you're wasting your time then."

"I'm not wasting my time. It's just a temporary block."

Jon got up from the bed and headed for the master bathroom, holding up his hand in a gesture of dismissal. "Right, right, I've heard that before. I'm taking a shower and then going to bed. One of us actually has to work for a living."

Hannah watched him leave the room and bristled at his tone, although she should have been used to it by now. Jon had been making snide remarks ever since she'd left her marketing job in order to focus on her writing full-time. He conveniently ignored the fact that she had enough freelance clients to pay her share of the bills. And that his medical school loans had always been the biggest drain on their income.

Not for the first time, Hannah wondered why she stayed with Jon. It was mostly out of habit, and the fact that moving out and starting fresh felt too overwhelming. She'd been with Jon almost as long as she'd lived in Massachusetts. She had met him not long after she moved from Indianapolis to Cambridge in order to attend Harvard. Jon had already been planning for medical school then, and excelling in pre-med, and she'd been drawn to his ambition and his confidence, two qualities she'd always lacked in spite of her academic success and admittance to the most prestigious university in the country.

She heard him turn on the water for the shower and forced herself to focus her attention back on her research. She hadn't wanted to admit it to Jon, but there was a reason she was having difficulty focusing on her writing.

It had started once she'd moved on to the Martha's Vineyard lighthouses. Hannah's family on her mother's side had spent summers in the island's African-American "Inkwell" community in the town of Oak Bluffs since the early part of the 20th century. Hannah loved visiting the island when she was a child, and had many fond memories of escaping the monotonous Indiana landscape and spending summers on the beach with her parents and grandparents.

Since her parents' sudden deaths three years earlier, Hannah had not set foot on the island she had once loved. It reminded her too much of her parents and, since the car accident that had claimed both of their lives, that was a door Hannah didn't want to open.

But if she wanted to write about the history of New England lighthouses, she could hardly bypass Martha's Vineyard. And she couldn't ignore the historic Gay Head light, which stood atop the famous cliffs of Aquinnah and was the oldest lighthouse on the island.

Hannah had always loved going to Aquinnah. She loved standing at the top of the multicolored clay cliffs and listening to the roaring surf below as the sun sank into the sea. Both her mother and her grandfather had loved the clam chowder sold at one of the small restaurants that lined the walk to the overlook. Hannah had never cared for the clam chowder, but loved the soft serve ice cream her grandfather always made sure to buy her.

Her family was all gone now. But the cliffs were still there, and the lighthouse continued to shine out over the sea as it had for centuries, warning sailors of the dangers of the cliffs and the rocky coastline.

Hannah's writing woes had started once she'd forced herself to delve into the Vineyard's history and visit the island's official website, which featured webcams of both the Gay Head light and the beach below it. She'd found memories in every picture and video she'd looked at on the site. Hannah sighed and clicked on the window she had been using to look at the lighthouse webcam earlier that night.

It was dark at Aquinnah now, and the night sky was lit by nothing but the full moon and the twinkling stars, as well as the lighthouse beacon, which rotated across the screen every ten seconds. A security light outside one of the restaurants cast a glow over the white fence and the stone steps that led up to the lookout area. Hannah stared at the screen and heard the laughter of her parents and grandparents in her head. She looked away.

As Hannah turned towards the window, a movement on the laptop screen caught her eye. She looked back at the scene beneath the webcam and was surprised to see a small woman wearing a long white dress walking up the steps toward the overlook. She was wrapped in a thick blue cloak and had covered her head with a drawn bonnet. The woman's dress was buttoned up to her neck and she wore brown laced-up boots. Hannah wondered what she was doing alone at the cliffs at night, hours after the tourists had left and the restaurants had closed. And wondered why she was dressed in such an old-fashioned manner.

Hannah watched as the woman stopped at the top of the stairs and looked back towards the road and the sandy path that led down to the sea. She stared out at the surf below her as the wind whipped her dress and cloak around her legs. She raised a thin hand to her head to keep her bonnet from blowing off. Hannah continued to watch as the woman started to walk again, heading up to the overlook and out of the view of the camera.

Hannah watched for several minutes, expecting to see the woman coming back down the steps and onto the screen in front of her. But the stairs and parking lot remained empty. Hannah wondered what the woman could be doing

9

at the overlook for this length of time. Unless something had changed in the years since she had last been at Gay Head, there were no lights at the overlook and, with the exception of the lighthouse beacon passing over them, the cliffs were pitch black at night. Why would anyone want to stand up there alone in the dark?

Hannah leaned back in her desk chair as she heard Jon turn the water off. She had almost forgotten he was home. She looked once more at the webcam, but saw nothing but the bright white beacon and the bushes that lined the stone steps. No one was there.

Hannah tried to imagine who the woman on the webcam was, and why she was dressed so peculiarly. Perhaps there was some sort of historical event taking place at the lighthouse that weekend. But Hannah had not seen anything about any special events on the island's website.

She closed her laptop and put her work away before Jon returned to the bedroom. She didn't want him asking any questions or making any more remarks about her book. Hannah left the bedroom and walked to the kitchen. She poured herself a glass of water and leaned against the sink as she took a sip.

Unable to stop thinking about the mystery woman, Hannah tried again to come up with a reason for her dress. Perhaps she belonged to one of those religious groups where women dressed conservatively. But that wouldn't explain what she was doing alone at the lighthouse in the dark of night.

Hannah realized it wasn't just the woman's presence that had seemed odd to her, it was also her demeanor. The woman was very young, but she looked overwhelmed with sadness. Hannah set down the glass, suddenly worried that perhaps the woman had gone to the cliffs to commit suicide. Was that why she'd never returned to the stone steps? Had she jumped from the cliffs into the sea?

Hannah didn't find that likely. The overlook was fenced in, and the ground below it was more sloping than steep.

Hannah shook her head and finished her water before putting her glass in the sink. Why was she trying to figure out what this woman was doing? What concern was it of hers, anyway? If the woman wanted to dress oddly and wander around the island at night, that was her business.

As she headed back to the bedroom, she could imagine Jon saying that she was fixating on this woman as yet another excuse to avoid her work. He wouldn't be wrong. But as she turned off the kitchen light she realized what it was that had struck her the most about the woman on the webcam. It wasn't just her dress or the sadness that was so plain on her face.

It was that in spite of the fact that she seemed to be so lost and alone, she moved with a purpose and sense of determination that was evident even through the lens of the camera. She looked like she was looking for something. Or like she was searching for someone.

1884

"*I* think he's coming 'round."

Christopher heard the sound of a woman's voice and felt a hand push his dark brown curls from his forehead. The gentleness of the hand was a welcome contrast to the searing pain that started in his arm and radiated throughout his body.

He tried to focus as he opened his eyes. The woman stood next to him, her hand still resting on his head. A man came up behind her.

"You awake, boy?" the man asked.

Christopher struggled to orient himself. He remembered the ship and the hours he had spent hanging on the rigging. The men who had rowed towards him and pulled him onto their boat…

"Where am I?" he asked, his voice no more than a whisper. "Who are you?"

"I'm the doctor that's trying to help you. Dr. Josiah Winslow." The man motioned towards the woman next to him. "And this is my wife, Stella Winslow."

Christopher tried to sit up and immediately began to cough. He gasped with pain. "Oh sweet God, my arm…"

"I'll give you something for that pain, don't worry." Josiah moved from the bed and returned with a vial of liquid. He stuck the vial in Christopher's mouth. "Swallow that."

The woman took a cloth from a nearby basin and gently rested it on Christopher's forehead. "I think he's running a fever, Josiah."

"Of course he is. Listen to that coughin' and wheezin'. He'll be lucky if he doesn't end up with consumption." He looked down at Christopher. "How'd you break that arm?"

Christopher closed his eyes and tried to remember. He felt a fresh blast of pain as his mind flashed back to the wave picking him up and slamming him into the rescue boat. "The waves," he said. "They tossed me into the side of the boat."

Josiah nodded. "Well we got it set. We'll do right by ya."

The man busied himself with a medical bag as the woman continued to press the wet cloth to Christopher's face and forehead. She smiled down at him.

"We will," she said.

Christopher noticed that the man looked more like the woman's father than her husband. He was more than twice her age, and had to be at least 40 years old. He also seemed to be nearly twice her size. The man was tall and heavyset, and he cut an imposing figure in a black woolen suit. He had thick black hair with a mustache and sideburns to match and brown eyes so dark they were nearly as black as his hair. By contrast, the woman was thin and petite, with small hands and delicate features. She wore a long-sleeved white dress that buttoned up to her neck. Christopher could see waves of auburn hair pulled back from her face and hanging down her back

He tried to lift his head and see if anyone else was in the room with them, but didn't have the strength. "The rescuers," he said, remembering the men in the boat. "Who rescued me?"

"Mr. Mayhew and some of the Gay Head Indians," Stella answered. "Mr. Mayhew is the keeper of the lighthouse. We're in his house now."

Josiah came back into Christopher's line of sight. "We set up a hospital here for the survivors, but you're our only patient." He turned to his wife. "I need to head back to Chilmark and check on Mr. Lambert. You keep an eye on this one here and give him more of the laudanum when he needs it. I'll be back for ya."

Stella nodded and pulled a small wooden chair up to Christopher's bed. He wanted to ask her what her husband had meant about him being their only patient. Had no one else survived the wreck? He was sure he'd seen another survivor on the rescue boat with him. And he remembered the men who had hung beside him in the rigging. Had they all fallen and drowned? Or frozen to death before they could be rescued?

Christopher wanted to speak, but he couldn't form any words. He felt so sleepy, and so very hot. His body was burning inside, but he was shivering as much as he'd shivered while he was hanging on the rigging with the frozen water drenching him. His eyes grew unbearably heavy.

The woman named Stella sat beside him and pulled a blanket up around his shoulders. He heard her softly humming as she caressed his forehead with the wet cloth. He turned his head towards her, and drifted off to sleep.

2013

"*I*'ve seen her three times now. It's so bizarre."

Hannah sat at the Red Sox Café and wolfed down her grilled chicken salad. She had been eager to meet her old friend and former coworker Sarah for lunch, and now that they were seated in the noisy café she felt as if she hadn't eaten in days. It felt great to get away from both her computer and her writer's block.

"Are you sure there isn't some kind of historical re-enactment thing going on on the island right now?" Sarah asked.

"Not that I've been able to find. And I would imagine an event like that would be advertised on the website. Plus, I've never heard of anything like that being held on the Vineyard." Hannah shook her head. "I can't imagine why she's dressed like this."

Sarah took a bite of her cheeseburger. "Maybe she's just very conservative."

"She must be. But that still doesn't explain why she's wandering around alone in the pitch black." Hannah lifted another fork full of salad to her mouth.

"You need to look at this webcam and see how creepy it is up there at night. The fog is so thick and it's so dark that I don't think you'd be able to see your hand in front of your face. I'd be scared to death up there at night by myself."

"What does Jon think about her?"

"I haven't shown him. Are you kidding? He's not even interested in my book, let alone some woman on a webcam. His eyes would glaze over the second I mentioned it."

Sarah shrugged and pushed her long brown hair back from her face. "I don't know why you two even stay together."

"I don't either. I keep thinking I'll move out once I finish my book."

"Why wait?"

"It's just too much to think about right now. Looking for a new place and packing everything…"

"When do you think you'll be finished with the book?"

"God knows. I'm totally stuck on it."

"What's got you stuck?"

Hannah shrugged. "More like what doesn't. I just feel like it's going nowhere. I think maybe Jon was right that it was a bad idea."

"Don't go by what he says. He's always been critical of your writing."

"I know but in this case I think he's right. I need something more for the book. Something to pull it all together."

"It's New England lighthouses. Doesn't that pull it together?"

"Yeah, but it's boring. I need a hook. Something more than just describing a bunch of lighthouses."

Sarah nodded. "I can see that. What kind of ideas do you have?"

"None. That's the problem." Hannah took another bite of salad. "So that's why all I do is try to figure out why this strange woman is wandering around the cliffs at night dressed like she just stepped out of the 1800s."

"Maybe you should just head down to Woods Hole and take the ferry over to the island. You could hang out at Gay Head and wait for this woman, then demand answers."

"How crazy would you say I am if I told you I've been thinking about doing just that?"

Sarah put down her sandwich. "I'd say you're certifiable."

Hannah chuckled. "I know. Don't worry though, I haven't turned in to some kind of crazy stalker."

"Good."

"But whatever this woman is doing, I'm almost certain it's more interesting than my book is right now. Can I help it if I'm curious?"

"Maybe you need to put this lighthouse book aside if you're bored with it. Try writing something else."

"I've thought of that. Like maybe writing about what this woman is up to."

"Hannah!"

"I'm kidding."

Sarah finished the last bite of her cheeseburger and glanced at her watch. "Yikes, I didn't realize how late it was. I need to get back to work."

"Okay. Thanks for meeting me. It was great to see you."

"You too. We need to do this more often." Sarah grabbed her phone from the table and lifted her purse from the back of her chair. She pulled some cash out of her wallet and left it on the table. "Do you mind waiting for the check? I need to hurry."

"That's fine."

"And don't get discouraged about the book. You'll come up with something."

"Thanks. I hope so."

Hannah watched as her friend made her way out of the crowded café and onto the equally crowded Boston sidewalk. She had worked with Sarah at Green Label Design marketing for years, and she couldn't deny that, while she didn't miss her job, she did miss the companionship of her friends and colleagues. Working from home had its benefits, but there were definite drawbacks, too. Especially now when she felt so stuck.

She toyed with the remainder of her salad and thought back to Sarah's reaction to her trip to Gay Head. Hannah knew the idea was preposterous, and she had no intention of stalking the woman on the webcam. But she couldn't deny she had considered doing exactly what her friend had just called certifiable. More than considered it, if she was being honest. She really wanted to go to Aquinnah.

****

"I don't care what you think of the idea," Hannah said to her boyfriend as he finished tying his shoes and stood up from the bed. She knew she had been right to not tell Jon about the webcam. If only she'd stuck to that decision. "I already knew you'd think it was stupid and nuts."

"Who exactly wouldn't think it was stupid or nuts? Besides you, that is?"

Hannah turned her back to him and returned her attention to her laptop.

"I don't know and I don't care. Why don't you just get the hell out of here? You can think about how important you are all the way to the hospital."

"If you're gonna be pissed at me because I think going to the Vineyard to stalk some poor woman you just happened to see on a webcam is crazy, I won't even try to argue with you."

Jon had adopted the condescending tone Hannah knew all too well. She couldn't wait for him to leave and was secretly thrilled he'd been called in to work for emergency surgery. Or maybe not so secretly. She turned back to face him.

"Good, because I'm not interested in arguing with you. Or even talking to you, if you get right down to it. I'm glad you were called in to work so I can have a peaceful night for a change."

Jon glared at her. "Remember who's paying the bills when you're enjoying that peace."

"Fuck off, Jon. You know I'm still paying my share around here. And don't get me started on how much of my money went to your school loans. Funny how you never seem to bring that subject up."

Jon turned and left the room without another word. Hannah heard him slam the door to their apartment and let out a relieved breath. She knew any mention of his huge medical school debt could always shut him up.

Hannah again wondered why she was still living with Jon. Or why he was continuing to live with her. Their mutual irritation with each other seemed to have escalated since she had begun her book project.

Hannah forced her annoyance and all thoughts of Jon out of her mind and returned her attention to her computer. She opened her browser and immediately brought up the Aquinnah webcam.

While it was a pleasant night in Boston, that clearly wasn't the case on the island. Rain pelted the camera and the limbs of the bushes that lined the stairs to the overlook touched the ground as the wind battered them. The stone steps were slick with rain. Hannah knew it wasn't unusual for the island to have different weather than the mainland. She also knew that there were few places more unpleasant during a rain storm than the Vineyard.

She stared at the bright beacon of the lighthouse as it rotated into view every few seconds. One white flash followed by one red. Hannah had read that the lighthouse had flashed three white lights and one red for decades, but had been changed to the current simpler beacon in 1989.

She knew this was the same time of night that her mystery woman normally appeared, but she couldn't imagine anyone coming up to Aquinnah in this weather at night. Hannah remembered being at the lookout with her parents when a sudden storm had blown in over the water. The wind was like nothing else she'd ever felt, and she'd had to hold her father's hand to keep from falling as they'd stumbled back to their car. She was sure no one would show up on the webcam tonight, but she still couldn't stop watching the page.

Hannah felt her heart pounding in her chest as she saw a solitary figure walking across the Aquinnah Circle road and heading for the overlook. She leaned forward and stared at the screen to get a closer look, but she already knew it was the woman. She wore the same white dress and brown boots she'd worn every night Hannah had seen her, and she was covered in the same heavy cloak. The flaps of her bonnet seemed to blow in the wind, but otherwise the woman appeared completely oblivious to the cold and wet weather. She stopped at the picnic table across from the steps and stared down at the surf pounding the rocks on the beach.

As Hannah sat in total silence in her Boston bedroom, she felt as if she could hear the pounding of the surf on the rocks along the shore. After what felt like an eternity, the woman on the camera turned away from the sea and once again headed towards the stairs. She quickly climbed them and stood right below the camera, glancing around at the empty stores and restaurants and periodically looking towards the red brick lighthouse at the top of the cliffs. Hannah expected her to head up to the lookout as she had each of the previous times she had seen her, but instead the woman continued to stand directly under the camera.

She grabbed her cloak and pulled it more tightly around her small frame, and looked up into the camera lens. Hannah sat back in her chair, dumbfounded. Surely she wasn't...

She was. The woman stared directly into the camera and right at Hannah. Hannah could see strands of auburn hair peeking out from under the woman's bonnet. The bonnet framed a pale face that was drawn and filled with sorrow. Seemingly oblivious to the rain around her, the woman continued looking at Hannah and, as their eyes met, Hannah felt as if all the air had left her room.

The woman raised a petite hand to push her hair out of her green eyes. She blinked, and turned away from Hannah to once more stare out at the sea. Before Hannah could breathe, she was gone.

"No, wait," Hannah cried out. "Where did you go? Come back, please!"

Hannah slumped back in her chair and shook her head at her own foolishness. Who did she think could hear her? There was no one else in the room.

But there had been someone else at Aquinnah. The woman had been there again. But how had she just disappeared so suddenly? Where had she gone? Hannah was sure she'd been watching the screen the whole time. She didn't think she had even blinked.

She refreshed the camera page and hoped for a change in the scene in front of her, but there was nothing on the screen but the driving rain and the blowing bushes. Hannah thought back to the moment the woman had stared directly at her and the two had made eye contact. Had that really happened? How could the woman have known that someone was watching her?

Hannah wondered if Jon was right and she really was losing her mind. She didn't even want to think about the fact that the woman's face hadn't looked wet in spite of the pouring rain. And, for that matter, neither had her clothing. It was as if the rain had no effect on her whatsoever. But how could that be possible?

Hannah sighed and let out a deep breath as she got up from her chair and plopped down on her bed. She stretched out on her stomach, rested her chin in her hand, and stared at her computer. She could try to tell herself she was crazy, but she knew she hadn't imagined anything she had seen on the webcam. She knew the woman had been there and had looked through the camera at her. She had purposely made eye contact with Hannah.

Had she been trying to connect with her? Send some kind of message? It had felt like it, but Hannah couldn't get away from the fact that there was no way the woman could have known anyone would be watching her. It was impossible.

Hannah rolled over onto her back and watched the ceiling fan slowly rotating above her. The timing of the fan reminded her of the lighthouse beacon rotating around and around, illuminating the ocean and the cliffs throughout the dark night. In her mind, she could see the woman making her way through the darkness and staring out to the sea.

She sat up straight and made a decision. No matter how crazy it seemed, or what Jon or her friends said, she knew what she was going to do. Whoever that woman was, she had made contact with Hannah tonight. Somehow, through the camera, Hannah knew that's what she had done. She was sure of it.

Hannah had to find out who she was and what she was doing at the lighthouse. She got up from the bed and went back to her computer to check the ferry schedule and make a reservation. She had no intention of wasting any more time. She was going to go back to Martha's Vineyard and to Aquinnah.

****

1884

Stella pushed back the green wool curtain and stared out the window of the Mayhew home at the steadily falling snow that had covered the cliffs in a downy blanket of white. Hearing a groan behind her, she let her hand fall and turned back towards the bed in the corner of the room. She walked to the bed and picked up a cloth from a basin of water on the bedside table before sitting down next to her patient.

She squeezed the excess water from the cloth and rested it gently on the young man's forehead.

"Mamaí," he moaned, as his hand clasped sheets soaked with his own sweat. He continued to repeat the word as if it were a prayer, never once opening his eyes.

Stella wondered what he was saying, if anything. Perhaps it was merely the gibberish of a feverish man. But the word sounded a bit like "mammy" or "mommy" to her, and she couldn't help but think that the man was simply crying out for his mother.

"Poor thing," she whispered as she took the now hot cloth from his forehead and soaked it again with cool water. She dabbed at his face and chest before returning the cloth to his forehead. She had no idea what else to do for him.

She got up from the chair and walked back to the window as the sounds of the fierce wind outside the lighthouse mingled with the soft moaning of her patient. The snow was coming down harder and it was now impossible to see the ocean beneath the cliffs through the curtain of white that covered the sky. There was no way Josiah would be making it back to Gay Head today.

The keeper's brick house, which was damp and chilly even on a warm summer day, was freezing now. The winter cold seeped into the core of the cottage and chilled Stella to her bones. Stella shivered at the chill coming through the old window and picked up her blue shawl from the foot of her patient's bed. She wrapped it around her tightly, grateful for the warmth it provided.

Stella had knitted the shawl herself but she'd never been able to knit as well as her mother. Her mind drifted back to another shawl of dark blue wool that her mother Alma Hammett had knitted for Stella when she was a child. And to the nor'easter that had swept over the island some years ago and left her family stranded inside their Chilmark farm.

She and her parents had gathered around the fireplace of their home, snuggling as close to each other as possible for warmth. Stella's dog Maxwell curled at her ankles, warming her feet with his thick fur. She had wrapped her thick shawl around her and leaned against her father's strong shoulder as he read aloud from the family Bible.

Stella could hear the deep and soothing voice of her father Charles as he read the ancient words of the Old Testament. She could see her mother get up from her chair to make coffee to warm the three of them as the fire crackled in the hearth.

The patter of ice hitting the window of the Mayhew cottage jerked Stella back to the present. She wrapped her shawl tighter around her and returned to the chair next to her patient, who had kicked his blankets off of his body and was now shivering from cold. But he was quiet at least, and appeared to be sleeping.

Stella pulled the blankets back up and tucked them gently around his shoulders. She listened to the howling wind outside and ached for the parents that haunted her memories. She chided herself for dreaming of the past. Her parents were gone and nothing she did could bring them back. She was a Winslow now, not a Hammett. And she was alone.

There was no one to keep her warm in the cold. There was no one to comfort her at all.

****

2013

$\mathcal{H}$annah leaned against the railing of the Island Home ferry and watched as the town of Vineyard Haven slowly came into view. She wore a navy colored trench coat that she belted tightly over her white jeans in order to shield herself from the wind that was an inevitable presence on the ferry, regardless of the season. She was grateful she had remembered to pull her long brown hair into a pony tail before she left her car on the lower level of the boat and ascended to the upper deck. No hair could withstand the onslaught of the ocean wind during the crossing from the mainland to the island.

She had slipped on her Indianapolis Colts cap for good measure and now pushed a strand of blowing hair from the rim of the hat. No matter how long she lived in Massachusetts, she'd never be a Patriots fan. The Colts were her team, which was yet another bone of contention between her and Jon. She tried to remember the last time they'd had a conversation that didn't involve some sort of argument and drew a blank.

Hannah pulled her cap down lower over her face and pushed all thoughts of Jon from her mind. She'd sworn to herself that she wouldn't think about him or their relationship while she was on the Vineyard and she needed to maintain her resolve. His openly scornful reaction to her trip was enough to set her teeth on edge, and she had better things to think about now. She was going to find out who the mysterious woman on the webcam was and she had no intention of leaving the island until she had an answer.

The ferry moved closer to the island, and Hannah could see the Stop & Shop grocery that greeted visitors as they drove off the boat. The famous Black Dog Tavern came into view, its iconic Labrador manning the docks. Seagulls glided alongside the boat in the hope that a few of the ferry's passengers would toss chunks of bread their way. As the horn sounded to alert motorists to return to their cars in preparation for departing the boat, Hannah took in a deep breath of the salty sea air. It felt good in her lungs.

Hannah buckled herself into her Honda Accord and, within minutes, left the Island Home behind and drove onto dry land. She drove onto Water Street and quickly made the turn onto State Road, heading towards Aquinnah and the Gay Head lighthouse.

Hannah was happy to be moving "up island," which was actually to the south of Vineyard Haven, because it was as far as she could get from Oak Bluffs and still be on the island. She had no desire to be anywhere near the town that contained far too many memories of her parents. While she'd always loved the Aquinnah area, she wasn't nearly as familiar with it as she was with the towns of Oak Bluffs and neighboring Vineyard Haven. The southern tip of the island was removed from the crowds and noise of the towns and therefore much calmer, which was exactly what Hannah wanted.

Hannah drove along State Road and passed the overlook of beautiful Vineyard Sound. She could hear her father insisting they pull off and take photos of 10 year old Hannah in front of the view. No matter how many times he'd been to the island, he was always the tourist, and drove her mother and grandparents to distraction with his insistence on stopping at every tourist attraction the island had to offer. Hannah could hear her mother chiding him and quickly blocked the voices from her mind.

She considered stopping at Cronig's Market to get some supplies and food for her stay, but changed her mind as soon as she saw the store's crowded parking lot. In spite of the fact that Memorial Day was still a few weeks away, the island was already bustling with visitors in anticipation of the summer season. Hannah wanted no part of it.

Hannah had booked a room at the Hammett House, a bed and breakfast about ten minutes away from Aquinnah in the neighboring town of Chilmark. She had read up on the house before making her reservation, learning that it had originally been built in the early 1800s by the Hammett family, who were sheep farmers. The house had now been restored and painted a beautiful shade of pale yellow. The Hammett House was surrounded by rolling green farmland lined with charming stone walls, and its secluded country setting made it a perfect destination for honeymooners and anyone else looking for peace and quiet. It sounded like heaven to Hannah.

Within a half hour, she had arrived at Hammett House and checked in to her room. She quickly unpacked her bag and hung up her clothing before sinking down onto the four poster antique bed and running her hands over the blue and yellow patchwork quilt that covered it. The room was a perfect combination of past and present, and of 21st century comfort mixed with 19th century charm. Hannah was tempted to curl up on the bed and stay there, but she knew she couldn't waste time. She hadn't come here for a vacation.

Hannah splashed some water on her face and removed her cap long enough to run a comb through her windblown hair. She grabbed a bottle of water from the room refrigerator and a granola bar from her backpack, and headed back outside to her car.

She opened her windows and let the cool sea air engulf her car as she drove the winding road up to the cliffs. The sun was just beginning to sink towards the horizon, and Hannah knew she only had a few hours left to search for her mystery woman before nightfall. She hoped to find answers at the Gay Head lighthouse itself.

The parking lot next to the stairs that led to the cliffs overlook was crowded when Hannah arrived, and she considered herself fortunate to take the last empty space. Getting out of her car, she turned and stared at the stairs and the webcam that looked down on them. She wondered if someone was watching her now from the comfort of their home, just as she had watched the mystery woman from her Boston apartment.

Instead of going to the overlook, Hannah bypassed the crowds milling around the restaurants and shops and headed for the red brick lighthouse. She knew the lighthouse was open for tours during the early evening hours, and she hoped to find a tour volunteer to speak with. All of the overlook businesses were closed during the hours she had seen the woman at the cliffs, but she knew that lighthouse volunteers and maintenance workers could be found at the cliffs at odd times. With luck, someone else had seen her mystery woman and knew her identity.

Hannah walked into the interior of the lighthouse and found a young man arranging brochures on a wooden table next to the door. He wore the standard Vineyard apparel of jeans and a faded hooded sweatshirt, and his long, stringy brown hair was pulled back into a thin ponytail. Sporting a Boston Red Sox cap and rectangular glasses, the man turned to look at Hannah as she walked through the door.

"Hi," he said, not even trying to be subtle as his eyes ran from Hannah's face to her feet and back again. Apparently pleased with what he saw, he held out his hand and smiled. "Are you here for a tour?"

Hannah resisted the urge to roll her eyes at the once-over she had received. She was used to being admired by men, and she knew she had received an excellent combination of genes from her white father and her black mother. With her tall and willowy frame, she had often been told she could have been a model. Her large brown eyes and high cheekbones added to her unusually good looks.

She smiled back at the man and shook his extended hand. "I'm not, but thank you. I just wondered if I could ask you a few questions."

"Sure. What about?"

"Do you know if there have been any historic reenactments up here recently? Maybe some sort of show or festival?"

The man put down his brochures and shook his head. "No. We never have that sort of thing on the Vineyard as far as I know."

Hannah knew that too, but she figured it couldn't hurt to ask.

"I've always thought those things were cheesy myself," the man said.

Hannah couldn't help but laugh at his undeniably Vineyard attitude. "I don't disagree," she said.

"Why are you asking?"

"I saw a woman up here recently that looked like she was wearing clothes from the 1800s. I thought she might be part of a reenactment troupe."

"If she was I've never heard anything about it. And I'm here almost every day now that we're gearing up for the summer."

"Have you seen anyone dressed strangely? This woman was small, tiny, really, and she was wearing a long dress and a bonnet. She had a big shawl or cape around her shoulders."

The man shook his head again. "I haven't seen anyone dressed like that. But maybe the woman you saw is a Mennonite. Or she's an Amish person?"

Hannah had wondered the same thing. But somehow she knew that wasn't the answer.

"She was walking up to the overlook in the dark," she said, trying another tact. "Have you had any nighttime events lately?"

"Nothing but the usual sunset activities. Everyone pretty much disappears as soon as it's dark up here."

Hannah could tell the man was starting to regard her with suspicion.

"When did you say you saw this woman again?" he asked.

"Oh, just the other night. I was hanging around after the sunset. Sometimes I like it up here in the dark."

She knew now the man was no longer just suspicious, he almost certainly thought she was crazy. No one would like being at the cliffs in the dark of night.

"I don't know what to tell you," he said, shrugging his shoulders. "Why are you trying to find this woman, anyway?"

"I'm just wondering if she's okay. She looked upset when I saw her, like something was wrong."

"Why didn't you just ask her yourself?"

Hannah knew the man would find her insane for sure if she admitted to only seeing the woman over a webcam.

"I just lost track of her in the dark. You know how it gets up here, especially when it's foggy. But I'm sure it was nothing." She flashed her best smile and reached forward to take one of the brochures off the table. "I'm sorry to bother you, thanks for your time."

"Not a problem. You sure you don't want a tour? The view from the top of the lighthouse is amazing to see."

"No thanks. I've already been up there lots of times. And you're right, it is amazing."

Hannah ducked out of the lighthouse and walked quickly back towards the road. She could almost hear Jon's mocking voice in her head. What exactly did she hope to achieve by this foolish quest? Did she want to make people think she was crazy?

The crowd at the overlook had grown as the sun moved closer to disappearing into the sea, and the sky had become a tapestry of purples and pinks surrounding the orange glow of the sun. Hannah climbed the stairs, her eyes purposely avoiding the webcam looking down at her, and bought a cup of coffee to go with the granola bar she had taken from her bag before leaving the Hammett House. Taking a seat on a nearby picnic bench, she noticed a man and woman holding hands as they walked towards the overlook. The man carried a young girl on his shoulders, and she rested her chin on his head. Hannah swallowed a lump in her throat and looked away as she sipped her coffee.

The granola bar and coffee were both long gone by the time the sun finished its slow descent and the crowds left the overlook and returned to their cars. Hannah remained at her table, determined to wait and see the mystery woman when she returned to the cliffs. Hannah knew she would return. She could feel it.

But she was wrong. The workers at the various restaurants and shops closed up and left for the night, and Hannah saw the young man at the lighthouse return to his car and do the same. The overlook was now silent except for the waves crashing to the shore beneath her.

She pulled her trench coat tighter around her as she shivered in the cold wind and waited. No one came.

Hannah glanced around at the shrubs blowing violently against the white fences and felt a chill that had nothing to do with the cold. This was not a safe place for anyone to be alone in the dark. Feeling like a fool, Hannah blinked back tears. She knew that both Jon and Sarah had been right. This was lunacy.

She got up from the table and pulled a flashlight from her backpack. Following the flashlight beam, she quickly made her way back to her car. Hannah felt safer inside the locked car and decided to wait a bit longer. But no one came.

Finally giving up, she turned on the ignition and drove back to the Hammett House. She was grateful to find the lobby empty as she walked inside, as she had no desire to speak to anyone and no interest in forced pleasantries. The night's chill clung to her bones, and the travels of the day had caught up with her. She was exhausted and wanted nothing more than a good night's sleep in a warm bed.

Hannah walked into her room and turned on the overhead light. Instinctively, she knew the room was different than it had been when she left. Someone had been there while she was gone.

She slowly set down her backpack and glanced around the room, seeing nothing out of order. Perhaps the maid had simply been back after Hannah had left for Aquinnah. But why would a maid return to a room where the guest had just checked in that afternoon?

Hannah's eyes zeroed in on the bed and the quilt, where she saw a sheet of paper set against the array of pillows at the top of the bed.

She walked to the bed, expecting to find an advertisement for the inn's services, or perhaps a breakfast menu. But she could hear her heart beating in her chest as she picked up the paper. Before she even read the words on the page, she was certain that the paper had nothing to do with the inn.

Her hand started to shake as she held the page in her hand. It was an old and yellowed newspaper clipping, an article from The Boston Globe in January of 1884. The headline screamed out news of a shipwreck that had happened off the coast of Gay Head two nights before. *The City of Columbus* had run aground on the shelf of rock known as Devil's Bridge, and at least 100 people had perished.

Hannah put the paper back onto her bed and sat down next to it. Who would come into her room and leave this for her to find? Was the Hammett House involved in some sort of presentation that was being held on this wreck? Perhaps someone had merely dropped the clipping. But why would that someone have been in her room and standing next to her bed?

She picked up the bedside phone and called the Hammett House's owner, Grace Pease. Pease answered almost immediately.

"Hello? This is Grace Pease."

"Ms. Pease, this is Hannah Forrester."

"Oh, hello Ms. Forrester."

"I'm sorry to be calling you so late…"

"Not a problem," Pease answered. "What can I do for you?"

"I just wondered if you or perhaps the maid had been in my room since I checked in this afternoon."

"No, I haven't. And Mrs. Rogers won't be back until tomorrow morning to clean. She cleaned your room before you got here today. Was something unsatisfactory?"

"No, no, everything was great, thank you. I just found a paper on the bed I thought you or Mrs. Rogers may have misplaced."

"What kind of paper?"

"A newspaper article."

"I'll ask Mrs. Rogers in the morning, but I can't imagine why she would have been carrying newspapers around while cleaning the rooms. Please accept my apologies, though. I'm sorry that a mess was left in your room."

"No, it wasn't a mess at all; please don't think I'm complaining." The last thing Hannah wanted to do was get the maid in trouble with her boss. "It's not a problem. You're just sure that no one was in my room after I checked in?"

"Of course I'm sure, Ms. Forrester. We respect our guest's privacy. And no one has a key besides Mrs. Rogers and me."

"Okay, great, thank you. I may have picked up this paper myself on the ferry or maybe back in Boston and just forgot, I'm sure it's nothing. I'm sorry again to have bothered you. The room is lovely."

"It's no bother at all. Please don't hesitate to call if anything else comes up."

"I won't, thank you. Good night."

Hannah hung up the phone and walked to the door of her room to double-check the lock. Maybe she had simply forgotten to lock it when she'd gone to the cliffs and another guest had entered her room by mistake. That was the most likely answer. Except that she knew she'd locked the door.

Shaken, Hannah grabbed a straight back chair from the dressing table and propped it under the doorknob. She returned to the bed and picked up the paper again. Grace Pease's voice echoed in her head.

"No one has a key besides Mrs. Rogers and me…"

Whether they had a key or not, someone had managed to get into her room while she was gone and placed the old newspaper where she was sure to find it. But who?

An answer crept into Hannah's mind, but she quickly swept it aside. She wasn't so far gone that she was ready to accept that. There had to be a rational explanation for all of this.

She looked at the paper again and knew where to start looking for that explanation. She'd spend the following day at the library. She needed to learn more about the wreck of *The City of Columbus.*

****

Hannah couldn't believe her eyes when she booted up her laptop the following morning at breakfast and clicked onto the official Martha's Vineyard site. She realized she wasn't going to be heading to the library after all.

There, front and center on the page, was an advertisement about a new exhibit at the Martha's Vineyard museum and historical society in Edgartown. The exhibit featured the most infamous shipwrecks in the island's history. Hannah had no doubt that *The City of Columbus* would be included. It had to be.

Stunned by the coincidence of the exhibit opening right after she had found the newspaper article, Hannah recalled the night she had decided to come to the island after her mystery woman had stared directly into the webcam and at her. She was shaken by the feeling that she was being led. But how could that be? And what could possibly be the purpose?

Knowing there was only one way to find out, Hannah quickly finished her breakfast and jumped in her car. The beautiful sunshine of the previous day had disappeared and she now found herself driving through a pelting rain. She considered herself lucky to find a parking spot near the museum, as the narrow cobblestone streets of Edgartown could often be a nightmare to navigate.

Hannah pulled the hood of her raincoat over her head and ran as quickly as she could to the museum, noticing the Fresnel lens of the old Gay Head lighthouse in its usual place on the front lawn as she ran past. She tried to recall the last time she'd been to the museum, and couldn't. It was safe to say it had been a long time.

She walked inside and shook the rain from her jacket as she wiped her shoes dry on the door mat. It was easy to find the shipwreck exhibit, as the museum was small, and a large banner hanging from the ceiling pointed to the display. The museum was crowded, which wasn't a huge surprise given the rain and nasty weather. There weren't a great deal of indoor recreational activities available on the Vineyard.

Hannah scanned the room until she found what she was looking for, which didn't take long. As the most deadly shipwreck in the island's history, *The City of Columbus* took center stage in the exhibit. A door from the ill-fated ship was encased in glass, and Hannah couldn't help but wonder how many doomed passengers had grabbed hold of that door as they tried in vain to reach safety. A builder's plate bearing the ship's name was displayed next to one of the quarterboards from its deck.

She paused at a display of newspaper clippings from the time of the wreck, finding coverage from The Boston Globe and The New York Times as well as the articles from The Vineyard Gazette. Hannah felt slightly lightheaded when she came upon the article that had been left on her bed back at the Hammett House. She didn't need to read that one to know what it said.

Moving on from the newspapers, Hannah was surprised to find photos and daguerreotypes from the days immediately following the wreck. While she knew from the famous Matthew Brady collection that photography had been available as early as the Civil War, she hadn't thought about it being used on an island as remote as the Vineyard had been in those days.

She was fascinated by photos of the Wampanoag tribe members who had manned the rescue boats after being informed of the wreck by the lighthouse keeper. They stared at the camera while holding the large oars of the boats in their weather-worn hands. Hannah couldn't imagine rowing a boat through the huge waves that regularly pounded the shore of Aquinnah, and wondered how the rescuers had managed to survive themselves.

Hannah's heart began to pound a rhythmic drumbeat in her chest as she came upon another photo, this time of two middle-aged men and a young woman standing in front of one of the boats. Feeling dizzy, she grabbed the railing of the exhibit case to steady herself.

"That's her," she said.

"Excuse me?"

Hannah jumped, startled to find she had spoken aloud. She looked at the woman next to her and pointed at the photo. "I'm sorry. I just recognized the woman in this photo."

The woman nodded and moved away. Hannah knew the woman thought she was nuts; something she was starting to get used to at this point. And something that probably wasn't that far off the mark.

But when she returned her gaze to the photo, she knew that it was the truth and not some crazy delusion. The woman in the photo was the same woman Hannah had seen on the webcam. She even wore the same long white dress and dark cloak.

Hannah looked at the card next to the photo and read the description. According to the card, the people in the photo were the lighthouse keeper who had coordinated rescue efforts and the town doctor and his wife.

Hannah cleared her throat and headed to the front desk of the museum, where an elderly woman dressed in a rose-colored blazer and a gray skirt greeted her.

"Can I help you with something?"

"Do you work here?" Hannah asked.

"I'm a volunteer docent."

"Can you tell me who the people are in one of the photos in the shipwreck exhibit? It says on the card they were the town doctor and his wife."

The woman followed Hannah over to the exhibit and looked at the photo Hannah pointed out.

"Yes, of course" the woman said. "That's Josiah Winslow; he was the doctor in Chilmark at the time and came to help with the rescue efforts."

"And the woman?"

"His wife. I believe her name was Stella."

Hannah stared at the photo and thought of the woman wandering around the cliffs alone at night. Stella Winslow.

She turned abruptly to the docent. "Can you tell me anything else about her?"

The woman looked puzzled. "No, I'm sorry I can't. What else is it that you want to know?"

Hannah shook her head. "I don't know," she said, knowing full well she sounded like a lunatic. "Do you have newspaper archives here? Or would I need to go to the library for that? I need to find out more about this wreck and these rescuers."

"I think you'd do best going to the library. They have all the old papers on microfiche."

Hannah nodded. "Thank you."

She got back into her car and considered heading to the Edgartown Library, but changed her mind as she turned the image of Stella Winslow over in her mind. The Winslows were from Chilmark, and the wreck had taken place off the coast of Aquinnah. She had already been in the right place when she'd arrived "up island."

She drove to the Chilmark Free Public Library and ran through the steady rain into the charming weather-stained wood building. She walked quickly to the reference department, and within a short time she had all the information available on *The City of Columbus* and the people involved in the wreck.

Hannah sat down at a table and ignored the incredulity that rang through her rational mind. How had a 19th century Vineyard resident managed to turn up on a webcam at 21st century Aquinnah? Hannah knew it was impossible, but she didn't care. She knew now that Stella Winslow had been wandering the cliffs for a reason. And Hannah needed to find out what that reason was.

She spread the documents in front of her on the table and found herself immersed in the Martha's Vineyard of 1884. Stella Winslow's Martha's Vineyard. As Hannah read through the materials surrounding her, she began to piece together a life.

1884

Christopher woke to the sound of his heart furiously beating in his chest. He felt an overwhelming sense of panic mixed with a crippling pain in his arm. Where was he and what had happened to him?

He blinked and glanced around at his surroundings. He saw a woman staring out the window of the room where he was lying in bed. Her back was to him, and her long auburn hair hung loosely down her back. Suddenly, he remembered. She and her husband had helped him after the wreck. The man was a doctor…

"Hello?" Christopher whispered, his throat as dry and parched as dead leaves. He made a painful attempt to swallow and managed to cough instead. "Hello?" he croaked.

Stella jumped and turned around. "You're awake," she said, her face brightened by a smile as she came towards the bed. She wore a heavy blue cloak around her shoulders.

Christopher nodded, afraid to speak more and start coughing again. The pain he felt with each cough was more than he could handle.

"Are you cold?" Stella asked. "Thirsty?"

"Thirsty," Christopher gasped. "Please."

Stella picked up a pitcher of water and a mug from the bedside table and poured Christopher a drink. She sat down next to him on the bed and held the mug up to his lips. "Can you raise your head to drink?" she asked.

Christopher nodded and lifted his head a few inches from his pillow. The slight movement sent a fresh wave of pain down his arm. He gasped and let his head fall back down.

"I'll help you," Stella said.

She leaned over Christopher and gingerly raised his head with her left arm. Supporting his weight, she brought the mug in her right hand back to his lips.

Christopher took several sips, wincing as the water went down his parched throat. He took a larger drink, grateful for the increased ease in swallowing as he drank more water. He took a last sip before motioning for Stella to take the mug away. As she moved her arm out from behind him, he let his head return to the pillow.

Stella put a cool hand onto his forehead. "You don't feel hot anymore," she said. "I think your fever broke."

Christopher tried to shift on the bed, and immediately groaned. "My arm," he said. "God almighty what happened to it?"

"You broke it before you were rescued," Stella said. "Let me give you some laudanum for the pain. You're due more."

"What happened to me?"

"You don't remember anything?"

Christopher watched as Stella measured out a dose of laudanum and brought it to his lips. He swallowed gratefully, desperate for relief from the pain.

"The shipwreck," he said. "I know I was in a shipwreck. But my arm…"

Christopher had a sudden flash of memory. A searing pain as he slammed into the rescue boat. Sailors pulling him into the boat and rowing towards the shore..

"I hit my arm on the boat," he said.

"The bone cracked," Stella said. "It's a bad break, but my husband set it for you. You'll be good as new soon."

Christopher glanced up at the woman's eyes, so green they reminded him of a forest. Or of the beautiful countryside of his homeland. Home. Where was he now, he wondered.

"Where am I?" he asked.

"You're on Martha's Vineyard. In the town of Gay Head. Your ship went down right off the shore below the lighthouse."

Christopher's memory started to return to him. "The lighthouse keeper. You said he helped me, right?"

"Mr. Mayhew, yes. He and the Gay Headers rescued you and now we're caring for you in Mr. Mayhew's house."

"You're Stella. Your husband is Josiah Winslow."

"Dr. Winslow, yes. And now that you've remembered us, perhaps we can learn about you. What's your name, sir?"

"Christopher Casey."

His Irish brogue became more pronounced as he said his own name.

"You're an Irishman, Mr. Casey?"

"That I am. From Galway. But I came to Boston last year." Christopher let out a deep breath as he felt the laudanum take effect and the edges of the pain start to slip away.

"Where were you heading?"

"Pardon?"

"On the ship. Where were you heading?"

"To Savannah," Christopher said. Boarding the boat now seemed like a lifetime ago. He realized he had no idea how long ago it had been.

"How long have I been here?" he asked.

"Two days," Stella said. "My husband should have returned by now, but the snow's stopped him no doubt."

Stella rose from the bed and walked back to the window, where she lifted up the heavy curtains. Christopher stared out at the snowflakes falling and swirling in the shrieking wind.

"The wind sounds terrible," he said.

"It's breezy," Stella agreed. "A nor'easter come up the coast."

Christopher rested his head back on the pillow. "It sounds so cold. I wanted to go to Savannah to get away from the cold." He shivered in the bed.

"You're cold now," Stella said, coming back towards the bed. "You may still have a touch of the fever. You've been burning up with it."

Christopher remembered the cough that had plagued him before he ever got on the ship. And his failure to listen to Mrs. Pitts' advice to stay home until he had recovered.

"I was ill before I ever got on the boat," he said. "Feverish and coughing like mad…"

Stella nodded. "You're lucky it didn't turn into the consumption."

She walked to the closet and pulled a thick brown blanket from the top shelf. Carrying it back to the bed, she opened the blanket and wrapped it around Christopher. "Get yourself warm, Mr. Casey."

Christopher nodded. "That feels good. Thank you."

"Are ya hungry?"

Christopher hadn't realized how empty his stomach was. He hadn't eaten since he'd boarded the boat. His stomach growled as if on cue in response to Stella's question. "I am, yes."

Stella smiled. "I'll be right back."

He watched her leave the room, her long hair swinging from side to side as she closed the heavy wooden door behind her. He turned back towards the window as he heard ice pellets hitting the panes of glass and the wind howling like wolves on the full moon. He wondered what the weather was like in Savannah at that moment.

Never mind that now, he thought. He should be thinking about all those men he had seen hanging on the rafters of the ship with him. Had any of them survived? He knew Stella's husband had told him he was their only patient. Surely others must have been rescued. Perhaps they had just been taken to another part of the island.

He leaned back on his pillow and waited for Stella to return. The room felt too empty without her, and he felt too alone. In spite of the fact that she had only been gone a few minutes, he missed her. He missed her presence.

****

"Our patient is awake, Mrs. Mayhew," Stella said as she entered the kitchen of the lighthouse keeper's home. "He's very hungry, the poor thing. I dare say he's not eaten since he boarded that ship."

"I've got chowder for him," Mrs. Mayhew said as she dried her hands on her long white apron. "And bread baking in the oven just now."

"It smells lovely," Stella said.

"As long as it tastes good, that's all we need to worry about."

Mrs. Mayhew was nothing if not practical. And that trait no doubt came in handy when running a house on top of a range of cliffs where her husband could be called out to man the lighthouse at any time of the night. Mrs. Mayhew seemed naturally calm and easy-going, although those may have been learned skills she had acquired to keep herself sane while raising the Mayhew's five sons. The youngest was now 20 and had married a girl from Chilmark the previous autumn. Like the rest of her children, he'd left Gay Head behind. Mrs. Mayhew didn't want to admit it, but she was thrilled to have the company of Stella and her young patient while they all waited out the storm. The house felt alive again for the first time since her youngest son had moved away.

"And what's our patient's name, Stella?" Mrs. Mayhew asked as she ladled steaming clam chowder into a large bowl.

"Christopher Casey. He's an Irishman."

"Would be with a name like that."

"He'd been living in Boston and planned to go to Savannah on the ship."

"Plans sure can change, can't they?"

Stella thought of all the plans she'd had for her life when she was a child. Yes, plans certainly can, and do, change.

"He's in terrible pain from the arm," Stella said. "I gave him some more laudanum."

"All you can do for him, poor child."

Mrs. Mayhew set the bowl of chowder on a tray and pulled her freshly baked bread from the oven. She noticed Stella staring at the bread with anticipation.

"Would you like a slice for yourself?"

"Yes I would, please."

"I could see your tongue hanging out for it. I'll cut you both two slices. You could use some more meat on those bones of yours, child."

"Thank you, Mrs. Mayhew."

"Let me get you some coffee now. I know that bedroom has to be cold with this breeze kicking up."

The woman put the chowder, bread, coffee, and condiments on a serving tray and handed it to Stella.

"There you go, girl. Best get back to your patient."

Stella thanked her again and slowly walked out of the kitchen, focusing on keeping her tray steady.

As she walked along the hallway, she smiled at the thought of Mrs. Mayhew. She was nothing like her mother had been, but she felt like a mother all the same. Stella enjoyed being in her company. It had been too long since she'd had a woman to talk to. Or anyone to talk to, for that matter.

She carefully opened the door and broadened her smile for Christopher, who had managed to sit himself up in the bed. It crossed her mind that she wasn't sorry the snow had delayed Josiah's return to Gay Head. She didn't miss her husband at all.

****

"We need to mend your clothes," Stella said as Christopher struggled to sit up in bed to greet her the following morning when she entered his room. "All that thrashing around on the boat tore them to shreds."

Christopher looked down at his shirt and pants and grimaced.

"I don't have any other clothes to put on," he said. "And I don't have a coat either. I lost it on the boat." He glanced out the window and shivered. "Looks like a blizzard out there."

"It's not a blizzard," Stella said. "Quite a breeze, sure, but it's just a storm."

Christopher stared out at the snow still falling and swirling through the air and shook his head. "As you say, Mrs. Winslow."

"I brought some of Mr. Mayhew's clothes for you to wear while I do the mending." She looked Christopher up and down. "You're not far off his size. And he has a coat you can wear as well."

"I don't know how I'm going to pay back Mr. and Mrs. Mayhew."

"I wouldn't worry about that. They're good people who want to help you is all."

Christopher winced with pain as he sat up and swung his legs over the side of the bed.

"I know you need more laudanum," Stella said. "I want to give you your dose before I change that sling."

"What?" Christopher asked. He didn't like the idea of changing anything about his arm.

"I need to change your bandage and your sling. Josiah told me I'd need to change it if he got delayed getting back up here. You need a clean bandage for that gash on your hand."

"It can wait, yeah? The pain…"

"It cannot wait, no." Stella busied herself with measuring out Christopher's laudanum. She stuck the vial in his mouth without a word.

While Stella waited for the medicine to take effect, she poured a pitcher of hot water into a large bowl and dipped in a bar of soap and a cloth.

"Once that medicine eases your pain I'll help you get cleaned up. You can't be dirty when you're fighting an infection. And believe me, that gash in your hand looked right wicked before we bandaged it."

She glanced at Christopher's matted curls and the mixture of sand and seaweed that was caked to his ear and head. "And besides, look at you. You're a mess, aren't you?"

Christopher chuckled. "I've no doubt I am."

He watched as Stella expertly folded out a new sling from a clean piece of cloth and set out an array of bandages.

"Are you a nurse for your husband then?" he asked.

"Not officially," Stella said. "But I've learned how to help. I like doing it."

"You ought to make yourself an official nurse."

"Like Clara Barton, you mean?"

Word of the American nurse's role in caring for soldiers in the Civil War and involvement in the Franco-Prussian war had spread all the way to Ireland, and from what Christopher had heard, the woman was an angel. He looked at Stella and found himself thinking the same about her.

"Maybe so."

"I don't think Dr. Winslow would go along with that. He'd surely say he doesn't need a nurse."

She sat down next to Christopher on the bed and washed his face and neck before starting to unbutton his tattered shirt. "I think the medicine should be working enough now. I'll try my best not to hurt you though."

"I can take it off myself," Christopher said, suddenly embarrassed. He used his good hand to undo the rest of the buttons at the top of his shirt and remove his suspenders from his shoulders. He pulled his good arm free of the sleeve and, biting his lip from the pain, grimaced and pulled the shirt over his head.

"I need to take that sling off for you now," Stella said.

Christopher cringed as she untied the sling and held the weight of his fractured arm in her hands. He moved as quickly as he could to pull the shirt off his arm.

He shivered from both cold and embarrassment as he sat on the bed wearing nothing but his trousers.

"I know you're cold," Stella said, "but there's no need to be embarrassed."

Christopher wondered if Stella could read minds in addition to being a nurse. "How'd you know I was embarrassed?" he asked.

"Because your cheeks are as red as the sun coming up over the horizon in the morning," she said, smiling as Christopher's cheeks turned an even deeper shade of crimson.

Stella rubbed the soap onto the wet cloth and gently washed Christopher's shoulders and chest. She struggled to keep from turning red herself as she ran the cloth over his pectoral muscles and her hand brushed the curly brown hair that ran in a line down the middle of his chest to his abdomen.

She rinsed the cloth in the bowl of hot water and soaped it up again, this time focusing on cleaning Christopher's unbroken right arm. She felt his eyes on her and glanced up into his face, blushing again as his chocolate brown eyes seemed to bore into her.

Stella cleared her throat. "I have to wash your broken arm now. I'll be gentle."

Christopher wanted to say he had no doubt of that, but he didn't trust his voice to speak. He cringed and let out a soft moan as Stella straightened his arm to run her cloth around his elbow.

"I'm sorry," she said. "I know it hurts."

Within seconds, she finished and bent Christopher's arm back into its set position. He clutched it to his chest as she used a towel to dry him off.

Stella got up from the bed and pulled a clean shirt from the pile of clothes Mr. Mayhew had given her for Christopher. She held up the white wool shirt in front of her.

"This looks like it should fit you, don't you think?"

Christopher nodded.

Stella returned to the bed and pulled the shirt over Christopher's head. He braced himself for another shot of pain as Stella pulled his broken arm through the sleeve, and then quickly finished putting the shirt on himself, using his good hand to fasten the small row of buttons at the collar.

"I still need to clean that wound on your hand," Stella said.

She got up from the bed, took a fresh cloth from the dresser, and poured hot steaming water into a new bowl. Sitting down again, she took Christopher's wrapped hand in her own and gently removed the bandage her husband had used to cover the wound.

"Do you remember how you got this wound?" she asked.

"I think it was from hanging on the rigging. I remember the cords cutting into my hand."

The gash was deep and oozing pus, and the skin around the wound was red and hot to the touch. Stella washed the wound and cleaned Christopher's hand, then reached for a small bottle of iodine on the dresser.

"This will sting," she said as she put the orange liquid on the gaping wound.

"I don't mind," Christopher said. "Compared to the arm, it's nothing."

Stella smiled and placed the medicine bottle back on the table. "Let me bandage this up again now."

She expertly wrapped the clean bandages around the wound and patted Christopher's hand when she had finished. She glanced back up at him and blushed again from the intensity of his stare.

"You're staring at me, Mr. Casey," she said.

Now it was Christopher's turn to blush. "I'm sorry," he said. "I'm just grateful to you is all. For helping me."

She smiled again and got up from the bed. "Just one more thing to do." She picked up the fresh sling and folded it into a triangle.

"We need to keep that arm tight to your chest." She placed the sling around Christopher's arm and tied it around his neck. "How's that feel?"

"Much better," Christopher said. "Thank you."

Stella glanced down at the tattered trousers Christopher still wore. "I can help you wash…"

Christopher cleared his throat. "No, no, I can do it, thank you." He raised his right arm. "I've still got one arm and hand to use."

Stella nodded and stood up from the bed. "I'll give you your privacy then. Once you're finished, you should try to get some more rest. Mrs. Mayhew or I will bring you your lunch later. And I'll get to the mending too."

"Thank you."

Christopher watched Stella leave the room and could feel his cheeks burning as he remembered her running the warm cloth over his chest. He couldn't deny that he hoped Mrs. Mayhew would not be the one to bring him his lunch.

****

"The snow looks to be done now," Mrs. Mayhew said as she set a plate of fish and a bowl of bread on the table. "Josiah should be able to get back up here soon I imagine."

"I hope so," Stella said, plastering a smile on her face that she hoped didn't betray her real feelings. She was grateful for every hour that passed before her husband made his inevitable return.

"Where's Mr. Mayhew today, ma'am?" Christopher asked as he took a slice of hot bread from the bowl. With Stella's help, he'd managed to come to the kitchen for lunch. It was a thrill to finally be out of bed and moving again. And it was a relief to be wearing his own clothes again since Stella had finished mending them that morning.

"He's over at the lighthouse cleaning the windows. No point having such a powerful lens if the windows are dirty." Mrs. Mayhew sat down next to Stella and took a piece of fish for herself. "How's your arm feeling, boy?"

"Much better, thank you." Christopher smiled across the table at Stella. "Although I'd hate to think how it would feel without Mrs. Winslow's laudanum."

Stella blushed and focused her attention on the food in front of her. "You'll have to thank my husband for that."

"Thank your husband for what?"

Stella jumped at the sound of Josiah's voice and looked up to see him standing in the doorway of the Mayhew kitchen. She got up from her chair and quickly walked towards him.

"Josiah! We didn't hear you come in."

Mrs. Mayhew also got up from the table. "I didn't know if you'd be able to make it up yet, Josiah."

"Of course I could. The snow stopped a good 24 hours ago."

Christopher stood up next to his chair.

"It's good to see you, Dr. Winslow."

"You look a grand sight better than the last time I saw you, boy."

"Yes sir. Your wife is a very good nurse."

Josiah nodded. "That she is. What's your name then?"

"Christopher Casey, sir."

Christopher thought he saw a sneer on Josiah's face as he said his Irish surname. But surely he would have noticed his brogue beforehand. His nationality couldn't be a surprise.

"An immigrant, then."

"Yes sir."

Christopher was certain now of the sneer.

"Josiah, you must be hungry after coming all that way in the cold," Mrs. Mayhew said. "Sit yourself down and I'll get you a plate."

"That's kind of you, Mrs. Mayhew."

Christopher watched as Josiah sat down in the seat recently vacated by their host. Stella did not return to her chair beside him. Instead, she walked to the stove and poured a cup of coffee, which she then set down in front of Josiah. He drank the hot beverage without looking at her.

"I'll want to take a look at that arm and hand of yours once we've finished eating, Casey," Josiah said. "Make sure my wife really has been a good nurse."

"Sit down, Christopher," Mrs. Mayhew said. "You only just got out of bed, and we don't want to send you back to it. You need to eat to get your strength back."

Christopher returned to his seat and felt Josiah's eyes watching him as he sat down. It was hard to believe he was still in the same kitchen he had been in before Josiah's entrance. What had been a warm and comfortable atmosphere just minutes ago was now filled with a tension so thick it was suffocating.

"What about you, Mrs. Winslow?" Christopher said. "Don't you want to finish your lunch?"

"Don't you worry about my wife," Josiah said. "She'll eat when she's finished fixing my plate."

Stella had returned to the stove, where she was filling a plate with the fish and bread Mrs. Mayhew had removed from the oven. She took the utensils Mrs. Mayhew offered her and walked back to the table, where she set the food down in front of her husband.

"Here you are, Josiah," she said.

Stella took her husband's now empty coffee cup and returned to the stove, where she poured him a fresh cup. She gave him the coffee and sat back down in her chair. Christopher watched as she pushed the now cold food around her plate and kept her eyes downcast.

Noises from the entrance to the home interrupted the tension of the kitchen. Mrs. Mayhew wiped her hands on her apron and looked towards the doorway.

"Sounds like William is back," she said. "But I wasn't expecting him to bring company."

Before she could leave the room, her husband appeared with a young man in tow.

"Abigail, do we have lunch for one more?"

"I'm afraid not just now, William. But I'll get something prepared."

The newcomer held up his hand. "Don't trouble yourself, ma'am," he said. "I've just come to talk to you all about the *Columbus*."

Christopher froze at the mention of the ship that had nearly taken his life. "You want to talk about the shipwreck?" he said.

"That he does," Mr. Mayhew said. "This is Arthur Chesham from the Boston Globe. He's been on the island and over in New Bedford learning about the wreck, but he hadn't been able to get up here to us until now."

Josiah got to his feet and strode towards the reporter. "Good to meet you, Mr. Chesham," he said, extending his hand. "I'm Dr. Josiah Winslow."

"Good to meet you as well, Doctor. I assume you helped treat the survivors?"

"You assume right, but it was just this one boy here," Josiah said, pointing at Christopher, who rose from his chair. "We didn't get anyone else."

"There were other survivors?" Christopher asked.

The reporter nodded. "The cutter Dexter picked them up and took them to New Bedford. And one of the lifeboats from the Columbus came ashore on the beach in Lobsterville. Three of the crew members were on it and they're staying with some folks there. But as far as I know you're the only survivor here in Gay Head."

"There was someone else in the boat with me. When I was rescued."

"That man died in the boat, Christopher," Mr. Mayhew said. "He was dead when we pulled you out."

Christopher lowered his head. "God help him."

"More than 100 dead is what we're hearing," Chesham said. "Bodies are still washing up and many have already been taken to the meeting house so their families can claim 'em." He glanced at Christopher. "You're a lucky one, sir."

"His name's Casey," Josiah said. "Christopher Casey."

Chesham nodded. "Then you're a lucky one, Mr. Casey." The reporter cleared his throat. "Let me explain why I'm here. I met with the Gay Headers who manned the boat and took some photographs of them. I'd like to do the same with you folks."

"A picture of us?" Stella asked. "Why?"

Chesham bowed slightly. "Pleased to make your acquaintance, ma'am. And you are?"

"She's my wife, Stella. And I'd like to know the answer to her question, too."

"Of course," Chesham said. "I'm writing a story about the attempts to rescue survivors when the *Columbus* went down. I'd like to include your care of Mr. Casey here. Frankly, I think you all deserve to be recognized. My readers will want to know about your efforts."

Stella pushed a wayward strand of hair behind her ears. "I've never had a photograph taken," she said. "I think it sounds like fun. What do you think, Josiah?"

"I don't see any harm in it."

Chesham smiled. "Great. I'll need you all to come outside. I know it's cold but I'd like to have the lighthouse as our background."

"I'll stay here and make you all some fresh coffee for when you get done," Mrs. Mayhew said.

Christopher stayed next to his chair as the others started to follow the reporter.

"Aren't you coming, Casey?" Josiah said.

"I don't think so, sir."

"Oh, please do, Mr. Casey," Chesham said, walking back into the kitchen. "My readers will be so curious about you. You're one of the only survivors of this tragedy."

Christopher's mind flashed back to his night on the rigging and the chatter of his companions in the Mayhew kitchen instantly faded to nothing. The sounds of dying men screaming for help and begging for mercy from the churning waters filled his head.

"It doesn't seem right is all, sir," he said, shaking his head in order to force the screams from his mind. "Seeing as how so many died that night."

"Please, Mr. Casey," Stella said. "I'd like for you to be in our picture too."

Christopher could feel the eyes of Josiah Winslow boring into him. He ignored the glares and smiled at Stella.

"It's hard to refuse a request from my nurse, but I'm afraid I have to. I'd rather just watch you all. And to tell you the truth, I don't think I have the strength to do it yet. Like Mrs. Mayhew said, I've only just managed to get out of bed."

"Suit yourself, sir," Chesham said, rubbing his hands together and once again leading the way outside the house.

Christopher pulled the coat Mr. Mayhew had given him from the rack in the hallway and draped it over his shoulders as he followed behind the group.

When they got outside, Stella noticed one of the rescue boats sitting in front of the lighthouse.

"I'd like for you all to stand in front of the boat," Chesham said.

Mr. Mayhew took a spot at the fore of the boat, while Josiah led Stella to the aft.

Christopher leaned against the doorway of the Mayhew house and watched as Mr. Chesham prepared to take the photo. The Winslows and Mr. Mayhew stood stoically in the wind as Chesham disappeared behind the cape covering his wooden view camera. Stella stole a glance back at Christopher, the hint of a smile on her face. She turned her head and looked directly at the camera just as a bright flash exploded from the box.

****

Stella picked up the container of boiling water from her cast iron stove and poured the water into her wash tub. Droplets of sweat dotted her forehead in spite of the cold temperatures outside. As far as she was concerned, her kitchen always felt like a furnace on laundry day.

She pulled her hair back into a bun and wiped her brow with her apron as she grabbed the washboard from the table and placed it into the tub. After pouring a small amount of the new soap powder Josiah had purchased on his last trip into Cottage City into the tub, she leaned over it and tossed his trousers into the steaming water.

It had been 10 days since Josiah had insisted she leave Gay Head and return to their home. She had expected to have more time with the Mayhews and to visit with the reporter and Christopher. But Josiah wanted to leave as soon as Mr. Chesham was done taking their picture. She had barely had a chance to say goodbye.

That morning she had been startled to see that same picture in the Boston Globe Josiah had brought home from one of his visits to town. It was surreal to see her own image in the newspaper she so loved to read. Stella loved nothing more than turning the pages of the paper and reading about the goings-on in the thriving metropolis of Boston. She imagined what it would be like to be in such a place, and wondered if she'd ever have the chance to visit the city herself.

Each time she opened a paper, Stella was grateful to her father for teaching her to read and to love the written word. She devoured every word of every paper Josiah brought to their home, in spite of the fact that he forbade it. As far as Josiah was concerned, women had no business reading the news of the world, and he scolded Stella for wanting to waste her time on affairs which were far beyond the capabilities of her sex. Stella pretended to go along with his order, but she stole moments to read the papers whenever Josiah left their home to visit patients or head into town.

Unsurprisingly, the latest paper was still filled with news of *The City of Columbus*. Stella read about the commendation Mr. Mayhew would be receiving for his rescue work and the fund the Gazette had set up for islanders to contribute to and show their appreciation for those who had risked their lives to help the ship's victims. She also read about the controversy swirling around the ship's captain and wondered if Christopher would agree with the accusations of negligence and incompetence that had been leveled against him. She wished she could bring the paper to Gay Head and discuss it with him.

And she wished he had agreed to pose for the photograph that now stared at her from the pages of the Globe. If he had, Stella would clip the photo and hide it in the pages of her father's Bible. It was the only book Josiah allowed her to read, although he never opened it himself. She could have kept the clipped picture as a memento of the young man she'd nursed back to health, and Josiah would have been none the wiser.

But Christopher wasn't in the picture, and there was no opportunity to change that now. It was foolish to even think of it. Stella had no time to waste on daydreaming, as she had to hurry and finish her chores before her husband returned home. Her mind wandered as she scrubbed, and, as she so often did, she thought of Christopher. She wondered how his arm and hand were healing, and hoped the infection in his hand hadn't spread. For a minute, her hands were running the warm soapy wash cloth over his bare chest instead of running the trousers along the washboard. Her face burned and her cheeks turned bright red as she remembered washing Christopher's muscular arms and broad shoulders.

She didn't even hear Josiah walking into the kitchen.

"You've not finished the washing yet?" he asked.

Stella jumped, splashing water into a puddle around the tub.

"I'm nearly done," she said. "Just finishing your trousers."

Josiah stamped his feet on the kitchen floor to shake the snow off his boots.

"Haven't I asked you to do that outside on the porch?" Stella asked. "I've just cleaned this floor yesterday."

"I reckon you'll be cleaning it again tomorrow then."

Josiah walked to the stove and poured himself a cup of coffee.

"A man can't warm himself up in his own kitchen?" he asked. "I'm trying to warm my feet 'fore I have to go back out and head up to Gay Head."

Stella stood up straight, dropping the trousers back into the tub.

"Gay Head?" she asked. "You're going to check on Mr. Casey, are you?"

"I am," Josiah said. "I imagine he'll need more laudanum by now. I've got Grover ready and we'll go up shortly."

"I'll come with you."

"Why? I don't need a nurse. You've got plenty to do 'round here."

"I never got a chance to thank Mrs. Mayhew for her hospitality when the snow left me stranded."

"I'll pass along your thanks."

"I'd rather do it myself. You know how I like her..."

Josiah stared at his wife over the rim of his mug. He did know the lighthouse keeper's wife was almost like a mother for the girl. She seemed to need that.

"Alright then, you can come with me. But hurry up and finish this here. I don't feel like waiting long."

Stella hurried to wring the trousers as Josiah left the kitchen. She tried to think of what baked goods she had that she could bring to the Mayhews. And to Christopher. What she had said to her husband was true, she did want to see Mrs. Mayhew and convey her thanks to the woman. But the person she really wanted to see was Christopher.

****

Christopher used his good arm to wash the windows surrounding the lens of the lighthouse, a chore he was happy to perform. He had grown weary of being treated like an invalid days ago, and wanted to do as much as possible to help Mr. and Mrs. Mayhew and pay them back for the care they had given him. He only wished he had his left arm to steady himself while he scrubbed, as he needed all of his strength to make the windows shine.

He had tried removing his sling a few days earlier while helping Mrs. Mayhew unload food supplies from the couple's wagon and immediately regretted it. The arm had started to throb almost instantly, and Mrs. Mayhew had tutted at him as she redid the sling and tied his arm close to his chest. He had faithfully kept the sling on since, as the last thing he wanted to do was go back to taking laudanum to manage the pain. He was grateful to be off the medication and free of the disorienting and mind-numbing effects it had started to have on him.

Christopher stared out at the sea below him and listened to the waves crashing onto the sand at the foot of the cliffs. Growing up in Galway, he had loved going down to the harbor and making friends with the fishermen as they brought in their daily catches. He loved the smell of the sea and always imagined getting on a boat himself one day and sailing away from the poverty and desolation of his homeland.

In the fantasies of his childhood he had never envisioned that the sea he loved so much would one day nearly take his life. While the ocean below him was calm this afternoon, with the sun sparkling along the crest of its waves, he couldn't look at it now without remembering the night the *Columbus* went down. He could still hear the screams of passengers and crew members alike as they disappeared beneath the roiling waves. And he could still hear himself praying to God that he would live to see the sunrise as he clung to the rigging in the darkness of the frigid winter night.

The memory brought a throbbing to Christopher's hand, in spite of the fact that the infected gash was healing well. He opened and closed his fingers, willing the pain to subside. It didn't.

He shrugged the pain off and returned his attention to the task in front of him. Moving to the other side of the lighthouse, he left the ocean view behind him and stared down at the rolling snow-covered hills and the dirt road that snaked through them, its path stomped out by the horses of the Gay Head Indians as they made their way through the snow. As he scrubbed the window, he noticed a horse and buggy coming along the road towards the cliffs. Surprising, as in the nearly two weeks that Christopher had been recovering at the lighthouse he could count on one hand the number of visitors who had come to Gay Head.

The buggy came closer and Christopher felt his heart thump in his chest as he recognized both the driver of the buggy and his passenger. Stella. He could see strands of her beautiful auburn hair blowing out from the edge of her bonnet and she wore the thick cloak he had seen when he first woke up from the wreck, frightened and in more pain than he'd ever imagined possible. He'd opened his eyes and seen an angel in a blue cloak standing over him.

Stella had rarely been out of Christopher's mind since she and her husband had departed the Mayhew home so quickly and unexpectedly following the arrival of the Boston reporter. While he was grateful for the care her husband had given him, he still felt a profound dislike for the man. It had been impossible not to notice the change in Stella's demeanor as soon as her husband had entered the Mayhew kitchen. It was almost as if he could see her spirit dripping out from her body and collecting in a puddle at her feet.

Christopher finished washing the window as the buggy drove up towards the Mayhew home. He dropped his now grimy washcloth into the bucket at his feet and placed the handle of the bucket at the elbow of his good arm. His wiry build and athletic body had always leant itself well to climbing, but his broken arm made it a challenge now to make his way down the ladder at the top of the lighthouse while carrying his cleaning supplies. He knew it was manageable as long as he concentrated on maintaining his balance, something that he was finding difficult since he suddenly found it impossible to concentrate on anything but Stella Winslow. He was grateful when he reached the bottom of the ladder and was able to switch to the winding staircase that would bring him back to ground level.

He left the lighthouse just as Stella and Josiah were stepping off the buggy and shaking hands with Mr. and Mrs. Mayhew. Stella caught sight of him and gave him a shy smile, and his heart immediately began to turn somersaults in his chest.

"Your doctor's here to check on you, Christopher," Mr. Mayhew said.

"I see that. Good day to you, Dr. Winslow. Mrs. Winslow," Christopher said. He extended his good hand towards Josiah, who shook it cordially.

"How's the arm, Casey?" Josiah said.

"Much better, sir. Thank you."

"I see William's put you to work."

"The boy's asked to work," William Mayhew said. "He's been a great help to us."

"Least I can do after all you've done for me," Christopher said.

"You know we've been glad to have you with us, Christopher," Mrs. Mayhew said, with total sincerity. She'd loved having a young man to care for, however temporarily. The keeper's house had felt like a home again.

"Could we go inside?" Josiah asked. "I'd like to take a look at the arm."

"Of course," William said. "Silly for us to be standing out here in the cold, isn't it?"

Christopher glanced at Stella as the group walked into the warmth of the Mayhew home.

"How are you, Mrs. Winslow?" he asked.

"Fine, Mr. Casey. Thank you."

Stella smiled briefly at him but kept her eyes downcast.

In spite of his genuine affection for the Mayhews, Christopher realized how much he had missed the sound of Stella's voice. His heart turned another somersault as he returned her smile.

"All of you make yourselves comfortable," Mrs. Mayhew said. "I'll fix some coffee."

"I need to go wind the clock," her husband said. "If you'll all excuse me."

Mr. Mayhew and his assistant keeper needed to wind the "clock" that kept the lighthouse beacon rotating every 90 minutes in order to maintain the rotation. It was a grueling job that required constant vigilance even during the overnight hours. Remembering the night he had spent watching the rotating light after the *Columbus* had gone down made Christopher anxious to help with this task, but Mr. Mayhew had forbade it. Only appointed keepers were charged with the maintenance of the beacon.

The Winslows nodded and took seats next to each other at the large oak table, while Christopher sat down across from them. Josiah stood up again almost immediately.

"Let's see the arm," he said, walking to Christopher's side.

Christopher edged his chair out and presented his arm to Josiah, who quickly untied the sling. Christopher felt a dull ache as soon as his arm lost the tight stability of the sling.

"Can you roll your sleeve up?" Josiah asked.

"I can, yes."

Christopher gritted his teeth against the pain as he straightened out his arm and did as Josiah asked.

Josiah nodded his approval as he looked at Christopher's bare arm.

"The swelling's almost all gone. Bruising's lightened. Looks good."

"Yes, sir."

"How's the pain? Are you still taking the laudanum? I've got more for you if you need it."

"No, thank you. I'm managing without it."

Josiah pulled a chair up next to Christopher and sat down. He unwrapped the bandage from his hand to examine the gash.

"Looks good here, too. The iodine helped ya."

Christopher stole a glance across the table at Stella. "Thanks to your wife's nursing skills, sir."

Stella blushed a bright shade of red, and Christopher regretted his comment as soon as he'd made it. He saw Josiah visibly stiffen at the mention of Stella.

"I've no doubt of that," he said, his voice now clipped and brittle.

"The coffee's ready," Mrs. Mayhew announced, breaking the tension that had once again crept into the room. "If the medical examination's over I'll pour you all a cup."

Josiah got up from his chair and pushed it underneath the table before he returned to his original seat next to his wife. "All done," he said.

Mrs. Mayhew set three cups brimming with hot coffee around the table before sitting down in her own chair.

"So I've asked Christopher what his plans are now that he's recovering," she said. "Not that William and I want him to leave us, mind."

"What are your plans, Mr. Casey?" Stella asked.

Christopher looked directly across the table at Josiah. "I'd like to do something to pay you and your wife for the help you've given me, sir."

Josiah raised his eyes as he took a sip of coffee. "Is that so?"

"It is."

"You know that's not necessary. I'm a doctor and you were my patient, it's as simple as that."

"But you went above and beyond," Christopher said, wishing he could say the truth. That it was Stella who had gone above and beyond. He wisely kept that to himself.

"Well what did you have in mind then?"

"I'm not sure of that. I don't know this island and I'm surely not trained in your profession. But I'm a good worker.."

"I can attest to that," Mrs. Mayhew said.

"I'll do whatever is needed, sir." Christopher said.

"He could help us with the farm, Josiah," Stella said, surprising everyone around the table.

"How do you mean, woman?"

"He could help with the sheep... I could use some help shearing them when the time comes. And he can help take care of Grover."

"Grover?" Christopher asked, wondering if the Winslows had a child they hadn't mentioned.

"The horse," Josiah said.

"He could help you with trips to town too," Stella said, turning to her husband and trying to keep the sense of pleading out of her voice. "You always say you wish you had someone to get supplies from town for you."

Josiah shook his head. "We don't have room for guests at our house."

"We have spare rooms," Stella said.

"You mean the rooms that are meant for the children we don't have?"

A wave of pain washed over Stella's face as she turned red and stared down at the table. Josiah had touched a nerve, and he knew it. Christopher was certain he'd done it intentionally.

"I could sleep in the barn," Christopher said.

Josiah let out a bark of laughter. "Used to those sorts of accommodations, are you?"

"Actually, I'm not." Christopher steeled his shoulders and met Josiah's eyes. "But I can make do with whatever accommodations I have. At least until I've paid off my debt to you."

Josiah set down his coffee cup and stared at the insolent young man across from him. If he wanted to work like a slave and sleep with animals, why should Josiah stop him? He could use the free labor.

"Fine then," he said. "You can sleep with Grover and the sheep in the barn and we'll have plenty of work for ya, I've no doubt of that."

"I'll look forward to it, sir."

Christopher took a sip of his own coffee and glanced across the table, his eyes meeting Stella's. The pain in her face had been replaced by the slightest of smiles, and her green eyes now sparkled with an undisguised delight. Christopher quickly looked away, but not before he felt his heart once again turning somersaults in his chest.

****

2013

$\mathcal{H}$annah rubbed her eyes and glanced at the clock on the library wall. 4:45. The library would be closing in 15 minutes and she hadn't learned a single thing about Stella Winslow and her husband beyond the fact that they had helped with the rescue of victims of *The City of Columbus* and, according to a Boston Globe article written by a reporter named Chesham, provided care for one of the survivors, an Irish immigrant named Christopher Casey.

Except for the name of the survivor, Hannah already knew this from her visit to the museum. As far as she could tell, none of the information she had gathered from her afternoon spent at the library brought her any closer to learning why Stella Winslow was now haunting the cliffs of Aquinnah and seemingly trying to communicate with Hannah.

Hannah cursed the reels of microfilm that were scattered around the table in front of her. She longed to be able to enter Stella's name into Google and discover all there was to know about her long ago life. Hannah hadn't realized until today how spoiled she'd become by the availability of online information.

She wondered if she would need a prescription for glasses by the time she finished scanning through the reels of 19th century newspapers.

Gathering up the microfilm, Hannah got up from her station and returned the materials to the librarian. She assured the woman she would be back when the library reopened in the morning and made her way outside, blinking in the harsh glare of the late afternoon sun. She got into her car and drummed her fingers on the steering wheel. At just 5:00, she didn't want to go back to the Hammett House and sit there for the rest of the night. That was a recipe for going stir crazy. But, she had no desire to make a return trip to Aquinnah, either. Not tonight.

Hannah chewed on her lip as she contemplated where to go next. Her stomach growled, reminding her that she had not eaten since the morning. Her mind wandered to her favorite restaurant on the island. But she didn't want to go there. Or did she?

Since she was a child, Hannah had loved going to Sandy's Restaurant in Oak Bluffs with her parents. Located right on the harbor, the restaurant was a quick walk from the family cottage. And, as far as Hannah was concerned, Sandy's had the best lobster rolls in the state of Massachusetts.

Her mouth watered at the memory of the rolls, and her stomach responded with a louder growl. Hannah let out a deep breath and turned the ignition in her car. She'd been determined to avoid Oak Bluffs while on the Vineyard but, after finding the old newspaper on her bed the previous night and spending the day trying to learn about a ghost, "up island" wasn't particularly appealing to her at the moment, either. And it wasn't as if being away from Oak Bluffs had kept her mind off of her parents. They were everywhere she looked on the island. Maybe it was time for her to face her own ghosts.

30 minutes later, Hannah was seated on the deck of Sandy's watching the boats come in and out of the harbor. There was something to be said for coming to the island in the off season. The lack of traffic and the nonexistent wait for

service at the restaurants was a welcome change from the bustle of the height of summer.

Hannah smiled as the waitress set her lobster rolls in front of her and departed the table. She took a sip of iced tea and bit into one of the rolls. The taste did not disappoint.

Starting to feel relaxed for the first time since she'd come to the island, Hannah leaned back in her chair and looked around at the town where she had spent so many of her summers. The Wesley Hotel stared back at her from its home on Lake Avenue, its huge porch mostly empty now. She knew that in a few short months the rocking chairs would all have occupants.

If she remembered correctly, Hannah thought the hotel had first been built in 1879 when the town was still known as Vineyard Grove, before it had become Cottage City in 1880 and ultimately Oak Bluffs in 1907. She wondered if Stella Winslow had ever been there. It was unlikely, considering how long it would have taken to get across the island in those days.

But maybe she and her family had traveled to the town to ride on the Flying Horses, a national historic landmark which had been moved from Coney Island to the town in 1884, the same year as the wreck of *The City of Columbus*. Hannah remembered the thrill of entering the carousel's famous red barn and choosing a horse to ride with her father. He had always managed to grab the brass ring for her at least once.

Hannah smiled at the memory, and wondered again if Stella Winslow had ever experienced something similar. It was hard to imagine the same horses that children rode today had once carried 19th century islanders around the same carousel.

The idea brought home to Hannah how little she knew about her friendly, or so she hoped, Aquinnah ghost. Did Stella and her husband have children they could have brought to the carousel? And what of the young man they had cared for after the shipwreck, Christopher Casey? Had they continued to be involved with him? Had he remained on Martha's Vineyard?

Hannah's mind wandered back to the photo she had seen in the museum and she wondered why Christopher had not posed with his rescuers. Perhaps he had been too badly injured. Although from the account she had read in the Boston Globe that did not seem to be the case.

Hannah finished her lobster rolls and shivered in the evening sea air. There were definitely some disadvantages to the off season, and the cold temperatures were number one on that list. Hannah felt the sense of restlessness returning to her, and she found herself anxious to pay her bill and head back to Chilmark. The ocean air had made her tired and she longed for her bed and a good night's rest.

As she walked to her car, her thoughts returned to the Irishman for whom she had a name but no face. She knew that Stella had wanted her to investigate *The City of Columbus*. Since Christopher Casey survived that very wreck, it seemed logical to assume that he was somehow connected to whatever Stella wanted her to discover. She admonished herself for not thinking of it earlier when she'd been at the library.

She got into the car and drove off towards Chilmark. At least she knew where to begin when she arrived at the library in the morning. She needed to find out what had happened to Christopher Casey.

****

1884

"*I*t looks like we're here, Grover," Christopher said as he nudged the horse towards the Cottage City Apothecary on Ocean Avenue.

Although he guided the horse, he had the feeling that Grover knew where he was going much more than Christopher himself did. The horse often looked at Christopher as if he was insulted that a newcomer would presume to know the roads of the island better than he.

In spite of his indignant air, Christopher had come to like Grover a great deal. In fact, he liked the horse significantly more than he did his owner. This morning was the first time Josiah had trusted Christopher to make a trip to town on his own, and he was grateful to be free of the man and explore this unfamiliar island with no company but Grover.

Now, Christopher and his equine companion arrived at the apothecary to pick up the medicines and supplies Josiah had ordered from the mainland. As Josiah had explained to him, he had previously always picked up his supplies in Vineyard Haven, the most prominent port on the island and part of the town of Tisbury. But following a fire last summer that had destroyed the main street of

Vineyard Haven, along with nearly all of its businesses, most steamers now arrived in the neighboring harbor at Cottage City while Vineyard Haven was being rebuilt.

This was fine with Christopher as he loved the strange little town with its gingerbread cottages and religious camp grounds. He looked longingly at the Wesley House hotel with its elegant awnings and huge wooden porch lined with rocking chairs. Josiah had informed him that the luxurious hotel had been built just five years earlier. Christopher wondered what it would be like to have the money to stay in such a resplendent establishment. He had no illusions that he'd ever find out, but even an Irishman could dream.

Christopher hitched Grover up to the pole outside the store and quickly walked inside to gather up Josiah's purchases. He was happy to see the friendly face of Eliza Luce behind the counter.

"Good day to you, Mrs. Luce."

"And good day to you, Mr. Casey. Where's Dr. Winslow today?"

"He's seeing patients at home today. Sent me to fetch his order."

"I'll get it for ya then."

As the genial shopkeeper disappeared behind a curtain leading to the back room of her store, Christopher glanced at the stacks of newspapers piled on the shop counter. Stella had slipped him a few coins that morning and asked that he bring the latest edition of the Boston Globe back to her. She'd begged him not to say anything to her husband as she read the papers without his knowledge. Christopher didn't like getting involved in secrets between a man and his wife, but he found it impossible to say no to Stella. It was a problem he'd had since he'd first met her.

He picked up the Globe and set it on the counter just as Mrs. Luce returned with several bundles covered in brown paper.

"Would you like to add the paper to your order? I know Josiah sometimes picks one up for himself."

"I would please."

"Did you see that headline about the doctor there in Boston who killed himself?" Mrs. Luce asked, pointing at the front page of the Globe.

"I didn't, ma'am," Christopher said. "I'm afraid I can't read the paper myself."

"Too busy working to go to school, were ya?"

Christopher smiled. "Something like that."

From his brief time visiting the apothecary, Christopher knew that Eliza Luce was in the running for the biggest gossip on the island, and there was nothing she loved more than discussing the latest scandals and rumors on both the Vineyard and the mainland. He could sense her disappointment at his inability to trade notes with her about this apparent scandal in Boston.

"Could you tell me what happened though?" he asked. "You said it was something about a doctor taking his own life?"

"Aye," Mrs. Luce said, with an unmistakable gleam in her eye. "Shot himself right in the head and left behind a wife and four children. With a fifth child on the way! No one can make sense of it. The man was well respected in the community and all of his patients loved him. What would cause a man to do such a thing?"

Christopher shrugged his shoulders. "Impossible to know, I guess."

"Some are saying it was gambling that did him in. Got himself in too much debt and couldn't dig his way out."

"I guess that could do it. A shame, whatever it was."

Mrs. Luce nodded. "That it is."

She packed the bundles of medications Josiah had ordered into a large canvas sack and handed it across the counter to Christopher. "Everything Josiah asked for," she said.

"Thank you, ma'am."

"Tell me, is Dr. Winslow feeling okay himself?"

"As far as I know, yes. Why do you ask?"

Mrs. Luce shrugged. "He mentioned needing some pain medication for a problem of his own is all, wondered if he'd injured himself."

"Not as far as I know," Christopher answered, admittedly intrigued. Perhaps the doctor had been so surly and disagreeable to him because of an ailment of his own. But Christopher doubted that was the case.

"Well, must not have been anything too serious then," Mrs. Luce said. "Do give him and that young wife of his my best. I never can remember that one's name."

"Stella," Christopher said.

"Ah yes, that's it. That little wisp of a thing. I don't know why I can't remember her. She's been here more than once with Josiah. I spose I've just never gotten used to the loss of Lillian."

"Lillian?"

"Josiah's first wife, may she rest in peace. I never knew a lovelier woman."

Christopher nodded, but the shopkeeper continued before he could respond.

"We never know why God sees fit to take the good ones, do we?"

"No ma'am, we surely don't."

"You best run along now, Christopher. It's a long trip back to Chilmark."

"Yes ma'am it is. Good day to you."

Christopher walked outside with Josiah's medications and Stella's newspaper and placed the purchases in the buggy behind Grover. He untied Grover's reins and maneuvered the horse back to the road before jumping up in the seat and urging Grover forward.

He winced as the buggy bumped along the uneven road. He had been going without the sling for a few days now but he regretted not wearing it for today's journey, in spite of the fact that he was unsure whether he could drive the buggy with one arm. He wished he had at least tried. His arm had been throbbing almost continuously and he longed to get back to the Winslow home and stabilize it with his sling.

The sun was starting to dip in the sky before Christopher made it back to Chilmark. He was grateful that at least the day was warm for late February. Winter had given the island a break since the blizzard that had left Stella stranded in Gay Head while he recovered.

As Grover turned onto the Winslow property, Christopher saw Stella feeding her sheep in the small field adjacent to the couple's house. Her shaggy black dog Henry, who seemed to be Stella's constant companion, was at her side. Christopher didn't know what kind of dog Henry was, as he was clearly a mix of many breeds, but he did know that Henry served no purpose as a sheep herder. He'd never seen sheep ignore a dog before, but that was exactly what happened whenever Henry tried to throw his weight around in the Hammett field. The collies that herded sheep with military precision back home in Ireland would have treated Henry with total disdain.

But that didn't seem to bother Stella, as she had only four sheep that she tended to, and she treated them more like pets than livestock. Christopher wondered how she had come to own such a small number of sheep, but he'd never been able to talk with her outside of Josiah's company since coming to stay in the Hammett barn. And he'd learned quickly that asking questions in Josiah's company was never a good idea.

He waved to Stella as he led Grover into the barn that also served as his bedroom. After filling Grover's food bag, Christopher rubbed the horse's nose and grabbed his sling from the bale of hay near his makeshift bed. He grimaced in pain as he sat down on the bale and smoothed the sling over his knee.

"I knew you shouldn't have driven all the way down island with your arm free."

Christopher jumped and nearly fell off the hay at the sound of Stella's voice. She hadn't made a sound walking into the barn.

"I didn't hear you walk in," he said. "You'll give me a heart attack to go with my aching arm."

Stella smiled and sat down next to him on the bale. "I'm sorry. I didn't mean to frighten you."

Christopher's cheeks turned red and he felt his temperature rise at the nearness of Stella's body to his own. He edged as far away from her as he could get without falling off the hay.

"I need to get this sling back on for a time," he said. "Stop this throbbing."

"I'll help you."

Stella took the sling from his lap and spread it across her own. She smoothed the white fabric with gloved hands.

Christopher's breath caught in his throat as her untied hair fell across her shoulders.

"Here," she said, as she picked the triangle of cloth up from her lap. "Let me tie this around your neck."

Christopher adjusted his body so that he was facing Stella's. He could feel her breath on his neck as she leaned in to encase his arm in the sling and tie it tightly to his chest. He wondered if she could hear the sound of his heartbeat.

She patted his arm gently and returned to a straight sitting position. "There," she said.

"Thank you," Christopher said, his voice coming out in a croak. His cheeks flamed red again.

Stella smiled and looked straight into his dark brown eyes. "Are you okay now?" she asked.

Christopher nodded, no longer trusting himself to speak.

"How do you like Cottage City?"

Christopher cleared his throat. "I like it just fine," he said.

"I love it," Stella said, her tone wistful. "You should see it in the summer. In August they have Illumination Night. Have done now every year since 1869."

"What's that?"

"It's a night when they light up all the cottages with paper lanterns from Asia. They're beautiful." While Stella stared at the brown wall of her barn, she seemed to suddenly be thousands of miles away.

"My parents took me there one year when Pa was able to get our neighbor Mr. Tilton to watch the farm for the night," she said. "We stayed in a cottage at the Methodist campground there with a friend of his, a minister who had moved to the town a few years earlier." Stella let out a deep breath. "I've never seen anything like it. It was magical."

Christopher was sure now that the sound of his heart beating against his chest could be heard far and wide, probably as far away as Cottage City. But Stella didn't seem to notice.

To Christopher's eternal gratitude, Henry ran into the barn and launched himself onto Stella's lap, giving Christopher a chance to recover his bearings. Stella laughed and buried her face in Henry's dark brown fur.

"You're a silly boy, Henry," she said.

"He's not much of a sheep herder, is he?" Christopher asked, relieved to find his voice was almost back to normal.

"He's not, no. His father Max was, though."

"Max?"

"He was our dog when I was growing up. My father used to say Max ran the farm more than he did."

"Your family had a sheep farm?"

"Yes." Stella waved her arm around the barn. "This was our farm, actually."

"What do you mean?"

"This land belonged to my family. The Hammetts were sheep farmers for generations here in Chilmark. But Josiah sold most of the land when we got married."

"What about the rest of your family?"

"There was only me and my parents. They died five years ago when I was 15. The consumption."

Christopher nodded. It didn't matter what side of the ocean you came from, everyone knew the toll consumption could take.

"I'm sorry," he said.

"Josiah and I married a few months later. He let me keep a few sheep but he sold the rest."

Christopher thought back to his talk with Eliza Luce. "What happened to his first wife Lillian? Did she die of the consumption too?"

Stella shook her head but had no opportunity to answer further. She jumped from the bale of hay as Henry ran to the barn entrance to welcome Josiah.

The doctor stared at both Stella and Christopher without saying a word.

"Josiah," Stella said as she made her way to her husband. "You're done seeing your patients?"

"Indeed I am. And where is my dinner while you're in here cavorting with the help, woman?"

"I was just helping Mr. Casey with his sling," Stella stammered. "I'm sorry, Josiah. Dinner is nearly ready."

"See to it that it is."

Stella nodded and practically ran from the barn, Henry close on her heels. Josiah stared at Christopher with undisguised contempt.

Christopher rose from the hay. "I've got your supplies in the buggy, sir."

"Not doing me much good in there, are they? When did you plan on getting them unpacked?"

"Now, sir," Christopher said. He paused as he remembered Eliza's question about his employer's health and considered asking the man if he was ill. It didn't take but a second to realize what a mistake that would be. He walked past Josiah and out into the now dark evening without saying another word.

****

A few hours later, Christopher sat up straight as he noticed flashes of light playing along the walls of the barn he was temporarily calling home. He relaxed as he saw the source of the light – Stella. She carried a lantern in one hand and a plate of food in the other.

"I know you must be hungry," she said.

"That I am."

"I'm sorry I couldn't bring you your dinner sooner. Josiah had some chores for me to finish first."

Christopher had no doubt that whatever chores Stella had needed to complete had been made up by her husband on the spot. He was actually surprised to be getting any dinner that night.

"It's fine," he said. "You don't need to serve me."

"You're our guest. Of course I do."

"I don't think your husband considers me a guest." Christopher said. "In fact I daresay he won't be requiring my services much longer."

"Don't be silly. You've been a great help to him."

Stella set the plate of fish chowder and bread on the bale of hay Christopher had claimed as his own. She had expertly balanced a mug of hot coffee on the edge of the plate.

"Are you warm enough in here?" she asked, shivering in the cold night air. "I could bring you another blanket."

"I'm fine," Christopher said, taking a sip of the hot liquid. "I'm used to it in here by now and Grover and the sheep are fine companions. We all stay warm together."

Stella chuckled and rubbed Grover's nose. Christopher couldn't help but think that she wished she could stay in the barn herself. Or perhaps that was just wishful thinking on his part.

Stella met his eyes as if she could read his thoughts. "I should get back to my husband now," she said.

"Yes, you should," Christopher said while wishing for the exact opposite.

As Stella started to leave the barn, Christopher suddenly remembered the paper he had purchased at the apothecary.

"Mrs. Winslow, wait," he called out. "I forgot your paper."

Stella turned around and ran back to him on tip-toe, her finger pressed to her lips. "Shhh," she said. "I told you Josiah wasn't to know I asked you for that."

"I'm sorry," Christopher whispered. "I forgot."

He stood up from the hay and retrieved the newspaper from his makeshift bed. "For you, madam," he said as he handed the paper to Stella with an exaggerated bow.

Stella giggled as she took the paper in her hands. "Thank you, kind sir."

She sat back down on the bale of hay and motioned for Christopher to join her.

"Did you read any of it?" she asked.

"I can't read," he said. "I was too busy working and helping my mam pay the rent to ever learn."

Stella turned to him, the light of the lantern dancing in her green eyes. "I could teach you to read," she said. "It's not hard. And you'd love it. I know you would."

As Christopher stared down at her the last thing he cared about was learning to read. All he wanted was to kiss her. He leaned towards her before stopping and scolding himself inwardly. She was a married woman. And, no matter what he thought of Josiah Winslow, he was a guest in the man's home. His mother would have been ashamed of him.

"What is it?" Stella asked. "What are you thinking about?"

"You," Christopher thought. *"How beautiful your eyes are. How much I want to kiss you…"*

"I was thinking about a story Mrs. Luce told me about at the apothecary," he said. "About a doctor there in Boston who took his own life."

"Oh my goodness," Stella said. "How terrible."

"Indeed."

Stella ran her fingers over the newsprint before folding the paper in her hands. "I shall read all about it tomorrow when Josiah goes to visit his patients," she said.

She got up from the bale of hay once more and walked to the door of the barn.

"Good night, Mr. Casey," she said, turning back to face him.

"And good night to you, Mrs. Winslow."

Christopher watched Stella scurry out of the barn and lay back into his bed of hay. He bunched the heavy blankets Stella had already provided around him and gingerly pulled his still throbbing arm closer to his chest.

He thought of Stella getting into her bed inside the house and wondered what that bed and bedroom looked like. He felt a stirring in his groin as he imagined what it would be like to lay beside her. To run his hands through her thick auburn hair and press his lips against her own. To slip her nightdress from her shoulders and take her small body into his arms. He knew it would be heaven.

But it was another man's heaven, and one he couldn't possibly have for himself. His face burned with both desire and shame as he scolded himself for coveting another man's wife. He closed his eyes, but sleep refused to come to him. He couldn't stop thinking about Stella.

****

Stella tiptoed into her bedroom and prayed that her husband would already be asleep. She heard soft snoring coming from his side of the bed as she removed her dress and long underwear, and dared to hope that her prayers had been answered.

She got into her dressing gown and pulled on the thick wool socks she wore to warm her feet. Blowing out the lantern on her bedside table, she inched herself into bed doing her utmost to not disturb Josiah. She slid under the covers of their bed and closed her eyes.

Stella nearly cried when she felt a rough hand on her shoulder and she realized that Josiah had not been sleeping soundly after all. He turned her onto her back and pushed up her dressing gown. Without a word, he climbed on top of her body and mounted her.

Stella gasped in pain as she always did when he entered her. She struggled for breath from the weight of his body on top of hers. As Josiah grunted and his breath quickened, she stared into the darkness and remembered the trip she had taken to Cottage City and the magic of Illumination Night. She imagined going on such a trip with the young Irishman now sleeping out in her barn. She remembered the day she had bathed him in Gay Head and run her hands over his bare chest.

As Josiah shuddered and rolled off of her, returning almost immediately to his snoring, Stella closed her eyes and prayed for sleep to free her from the confines of both her bedroom and her life. When it did, she dreamed of Christopher.

****

"So you've never sheared a sheep?" Stella asked as she and Christopher walked out of the barn and into the bright sunshine of the surprisingly warm March morning. Henry the dog ran along beside them.

"Can't say that I have."

"No sheep farmers in Galway then?"

"No, there were. But I spent all of my time down at the harbor."

"Was your father a seaman?"

Christopher shrugged his shoulders. "I really can't say what he was. He died before I was born."

Stella stopped walking. "I'm sorry."

"Don't be. It's not as if I ever knew the man."

"What happened to him?"

"I can't say that for sure, either. My mam told me he died after a fall, but she wouldn't say more. When I got older, other children teased me and said my father was a drunk who fell into the sea, that's what their parents told them. But when I asked my mam if that was the truth, she said I shouldn't listen to idiots."

"Do you think it was the truth?"

"I do, yeah." Christopher lifted his head to the sky and soaked in the rays of the sun on his pale face. "I think my mam just believed that you shouldn't speak ill of the dead."

"A wise woman."

"That she was."

"Was?"

Christopher looked back towards Stella. "Yes. She died three years ago; two days shy of my 18th birthday."

Stella noticed a wave of darkness pass over Christopher's pale face. "I'm sorry."

"Thank you."

"What happened to her?"

"She was caught in a kitchen fire at the home where she worked as a cook. The fire spread fast as lightening and she couldn't get out in time."

"How terrible."

"It was."

Stella suddenly remembered the word Christopher had moaned in his feverish sleep while she cared for him at the Mayhew home.

"When we were at the Mayhew's cottage and you were sick with fever, you said a word over and over again," she said. "Mamaí. Does that mean mother? Were you asking for her?"

Christopher's face whitened. "I must have been. That was what I called her, yes. It's Gaelic for mother."

"Gaelic?"

"The Irish language. It's illegal to speak it now in Ireland because of the English, but my mam taught me anyway. We just always made sure never to speak it to anyone else. It was our secret we had, she and I." He glanced at Stella, his eyes clouded with pain. "I haven't spoken it since she died."

"I thought the word sounded lovely," she said.

"It's a lovely language." Christopher smiled down at Stella. "Do you know what you are in Gaelic?"

"What?"

"Cailín álainn."

"What's that?"

Christopher grinned. "I won't tell."

Stella laughed. "That's not fair. How do I know you didn't say I'm something scary or ugly? Maybe a witch or a hag?"

"Trust me, you are neither."

"It's not fair for you not to tell me what you said," Stella said again.

"There are lots of things in life that aren't fair."

Stella laughed and leaned against the fence surrounding her sheep. She'd nearly forgotten the reason she had come outside was to show Christopher how to shear them.

"I'm glad Josiah had to go care for a patient this morning," she said, to her own surprise. She turned bright red and stared at the ground. "Please forgive me, I never should have said such a thing. I don't know what came over me."

"It's alright."

"No, it isn't. I've no right to talk of my husband that way. I can't imagine what you must think of me."

"I think very highly of you. Always have."

Stella turned away from him, and Christopher was sure he saw the glint of a tear in her eye.

"Your husband doesn't treat you very kindly, does he?"

Stella turned back around. "Why do you say that? Josiah has always taken care of me."

"Why did you marry him?"

"What do you mean why did I marry him? Why does any woman marry a man?" Stella stepped back and squared her shoulders. "Listen, Mr. Casey, I do apologize for my earlier words. I'd never criticize my husband. I'm sure now I've given you the wrong impression."

"And I apologize for offending you, Mrs. Winslow. You and your husband have been very kind to me. Forgive me, please."

Stella cleared her throat. "I do forgive you, and again ask for your forgiveness as well." She opened the gate of the field and stepped inside, Henry at her heels. "Shall we get to the sheep now? I fear we've wasted enough time already."

Christopher bowed slightly and followed her through the gate. "I'm at your service."

****

Josiah pulled Grover over to the side of the road in front of his home and watched Stella attempting to teach the Irishman how to shear a sheep. The sheep kicked Casey with both hind legs and wiggled out of his grasp, which caused him to fall on his rear end as the sheep galloped to the other end of the field. Josiah seethed as he watched Stella laugh so hard she was doubled over and clutching at her stomach with one hand while clutching the fence post with the other to keep her balance.

He couldn't remember when he'd last seen her smile, let alone laugh. To him, she was a sour and morose child. Her attitude only made him miss his real wife Lillian more.

But apparently the only thing his current wife needed to change her demeanor and make her happy was a strapping young man in her company. He'd always felt twice his age around Stella and regretted more than once his decision to marry her when he needed a wife and she needed someone to take care of her. What had he been thinking, marrying a 15 year old girl at his age?

Josiah knew he'd let his good feelings for Stella's parents get in the way of his common sense. But in spite of her young age, he'd never imagined she'd make a fool out of him by throwing herself at this mucker who washed up onto their island uninvited and unwanted. He'd had a duty as a doctor to care for the boy, but he'd never intended to bring him into his life and home. Not even in the barn. And he'd certainly never expected to find his wife cavorting with him. He'd thought Stella's parents had raised her better.

Josiah sighed and rubbed his hand along Grover's mane. It was just one more in a long line of disappointments in his marriage. Stella was nothing like his beloved Lillian, a God fearing woman of taste and discretion. Josiah himself would never forgive God for taking Lillian away from him.

He winced as he heard the sounds of Stella and Christopher laughing together now as the boy finally managed to hold on to the sheep long enough to shear off a length of wool from its body. He scowled, wondering why he had ever even agreed to let Stella keep the damn sheep. She didn't make enough from the small amount of wool she sold to make them worthwhile. He'd been a fool to go along with her sentimental attachment to the damn animals. He needed to rectify that mistake.

Josiah shifted on his saddle and winced again, this time in pain. He knew his condition was getting worse, and he wanted Casey to go to town at least one more time to get him a fresh supply of pain medication. He didn't know if he still had it in him to make the trip clear across the island.

After that though, Christopher Casey needed to vacate his premises. He'd had enough of this foolishness to last whatever lifetime was left to him. And he wanted the boy gone before the spring came and more neighbors would be about. He could only imagine the talk if anyone else saw Stella carrying on like this. He'd be damned if he'd allow his name to be the subject of island gossip.

Josiah gritted his teeth and maneuvered Grover into the drive of his home. He saw the smile leave Stella's face the instant she noticed him. The sound of laughter immediately died as both she and Casey turned and watched him come towards them.

Josiah took some satisfaction in knowing his return had spoiled his wife's fun. She'd made him miserable long enough. It was high time he returned the favor.

****

A week passed before Josiah made good on his promise to make his wife miserable. He waited for Stella to retire to bed for the night, then grabbed a lantern and headed outside to the barn. He found Christopher talking to Grover and nuzzling the horse's snout.

"Trying to take my horse from me, Casey?" Josiah asked.

Christopher jumped, startled at Josiah's interruption. "I hadn't realized you'd come in the barn, Doctor Winslow. Do you need something?"

"How about an answer to my question to start."

"About Grover? He's a fine horse, no question. I can't deny I've become fond of him." Christopher forced a smile onto his face. "We've become friends sharing our living quarters."

Josiah stared at Christopher with undisguised hatred.

"Is there something I can do for you, Doctor?" Christopher asked. "Did you get the bundles I picked up for you at the apothecary today?"

"I did get my order, yes. What business are those bundles of yours, boy?"

"No business at all. I just thought perhaps there was a problem."

"And what makes you think I have a problem?"

It was clear to Christopher that Josiah was not interested in a logical conversation. He cleared his throat and tried to defuse what had become an unexpectedly tense situation.

"I don't, sir. My apologies if I misspoke. What can I do for you?"

"What you can do is remove yourself from my property. Your debt is paid here."

Christopher was disheartened to hear this but not entirely surprised. He knew Josiah wouldn't keep him around forever, in spite of the free labor he was getting. He'd never hidden his feelings about his former patient, although Christopher had never understood what he'd done to offend the man.

"I understand," he said. "I'm grateful for the opportunity you've given me to make reparations to you and your wife. I'll make arrangements to leave and will be gone as soon as possible."

"You'll be gone now."

"Sir?"

"You heard me. I want you gone now."

"In the dead of night? It's pitch black outside."

"Are you afraid of the dark?"

"No sir, but.."

"No buts. This is my home and I make the rules." Josiah glanced around the barn. "It's not as if you have anything to pack up, is it? So get out. Off my property and out of my home." Josiah sneered. "And away from my wife."

Christopher tried unsuccessfully to swallow his anger. "That's what this is about then? Mrs. Winslow?"

"It's not about anything but the fact that I've had enough of you and I want you off my land. I don't need a squatter here." Josiah turned away and waved his hand in a gesture of dismissal. "You wanted to make amends to me and you have. Now get out. I don't want to see you here in the morning."

Josiah departed the barn, but not before he grabbed Christopher's lantern and carried it out with him. Christopher fumbled in the dark trying to find the hat and gloves Mr. Mayhew had given him. He'd need all the warmth he could get out on the road at this hour.

He wanted to take the blanket Stella had given him along, but resisted the urge to do so. As angry as Josiah was, it wasn't difficult to imagine him accusing Christopher of stealing. Christopher buttoned up his coat and tried to glance around the barn. He could no longer see the horse, but he could hear him.

"Goodbye, Grover," he said into the dark. "You're a much better fellow than your owner."

The horse whinnied and stomped the ground with his hoof in response.

Christopher walked outside into the night and lifted the collar of his coat up around his neck. Although it was cold enough for his breath to be visible in the frigid air, he was in luck as the night sky was crystal clear and the blanket of stars provided more light than he expected. He walked to the road and looked back at the house noticing a lantern go out in the bedroom window. Josiah had obviously retired for the night.

Christopher felt a pang of jealousy as he imagined Josiah warm in bed beside Stella. He wondered if Stella knew of Josiah's decision to get rid of him. He couldn't say for sure, of course, but he liked to believe she didn't.

He looked up and down the empty road and wondered which way to turn. As always, he felt drawn to the sea. He'd heard Stella talking of the harbor in Chilmark called Menemsha, and he wondered if it was similar to his home of Galway and the harbor he loved. He didn't know where Menemsha was, but he knew one direction led "down island" towards the towns of Cottage City and Edgartown. Since he'd never come upon Menemsha in his travels that way for

Josiah, it was logical to assume the other direction was the way to go. If nothing else, he'd eventually find his way back to Mr. and Mrs. Mayhew and Aquinnah.

Christopher took one last look back at the Winslow house and said a silent goodbye to the beautiful girl inside. The "cailín álainn," as he'd called her. He wondered if she'd ever learn what he'd meant. He doubted it, as it was unlikely to find any other Gaelic speakers on this overwhelmingly Anglo island.

He walked out onto the road and headed towards what he hoped was Menemsha, walking quickly to keep warm and in the hopes that he'd make it to his destination by daylight. He felt sure he'd never see his "cailín álainn" Stella Winslow again.

****

"Good morning, Josiah," Stella said as she prepared breakfast. "Did you sleep well?"

"I did," Josiah said, sitting down at the table. "Better than I have in a long time."

"I'm glad for that. I've got coffee ready for you."

Stella moved to the table and poured a cup of hot coffee for her husband. She removed two additional mugs from her cabinet and set them on the table next to her plate.

"Are you expecting company?" Josiah asked.

"Why do you ask?" Stella asked, confused.

"Do you need two mugs of coffee for yourself?"

Stella looked at the mugs in front of her still puzzled. "No, of course not. I've just got this down for Mr. Casey. I bring him his breakfast after we eat. You know that."

Josiah shook his head as he took a sip of coffee. "You won't need to be doing that any more. Mr. Casey is no longer staying with us."

"What do you mean? What's happened to him?"

"Nothing's happened to him. I sent him on his way is all. He'd paid off his debt and I told him so."

Stella suddenly felt unable to breathe. "He was here last night. I brought him dinner when he returned from picking up the medicines you ordered."

"I'm well aware of that. I told him to leave before I came to bed."

"You told him to leave in the night?"

"I did. I saw no reason to wait."

Stella grabbed the edge of the table and tried to steady herself. "You saw no reason? The fact that it was the middle of the night isn't a reason?"

"You think a man is too fragile to walk in the dark?" Josiah slammed down his mug. "Are you going to get my breakfast or am I to survive on coffee only this morning?"

"I don't care what you survive on."

Josiah stood up from his chair and towered over Stella with his bulk. "Don't you take that tone with me."

"I'll take any tone I please. How could you do this?"

Josiah sneered. "Do what? Settle my accounts with a lodger and former patient? I wasn't aware I needed to consult you on my business affairs."

"It wasn't a business matter. You hated Mr. Casey and you never pretended otherwise. Why else would you send him out into the night with nothing? On an island where he's a stranger? God in heaven, what's become of you? My father wouldn't believe it."

Josiah grabbed Stella's arm and twisted it towards her back pinning her up against the table.

"You're hurting me," she gasped.

"Damn right I am. You're not to question me again, do I make myself clear? You watch yourself, woman." He twisted the arm again and tightened his grip.

"Stop," Stella said. "Please."

"It's interesting that you're so aghast at the fact that young Mr. Casey isn't here anymore. Do you think I'm a fool? Or blind? Do you think I couldn't see the way you threw yourself at him like one of your damn sheep in heat?"

"I didn't," Stella pleaded. "Josiah, please. You'll break my arm."

Josiah gave one last twist and let go, pushing Stella towards the wall of the kitchen. She stumbled and grabbed the table to maintain her balance. Tears sprung from her eyes as she cradled her arm against her chest.

"I won't allow you to make a fool of me," Josiah said, wagging his finger in Stella's face. "You'll do well to remember you're a married woman."

"I wasn't doing anything against you," Stella said. "Mr. Casey was a friend to me, that's all."

"That's all, is it? You must think I was born yesterday, you stupid girl." He started to reach for her again, but Stella backed out of his reach.

"Josiah, please. I haven't done anything to make a fool of you."

Josiah stared at his wife and felt his anger rising in his chest. He fought the urge to strike her and beat whatever fantasies she'd had about that damn Irishman out of her. Instead, he backed away and sat back down at the table, where he calmly took a sip of coffee.

"The coffee's gone cold," he said. "You'll need to make another pot."

Stella returned to her stove with shaking hands. She grasped onto the stove and took a deep breath to steady herself.

"I'll have it ready in a moment, Josiah," she said.

Stella rubbed the tears from her face and set about making a new pot of coffee.

****

Christopher hauled the net of clams from Mr. Lambert's boat and tossed it onto the dock next to the rest of the day's catch. Sweating in the bright sun of the early spring day, he took off his oil-cloth coat and stepped out of the water-repellant pants he had worn on the boat. It felt good to be out of the cumbersome clothing now that he was back on dry land.

Rolling up his shirt sleeves, Christopher grabbed the clams and carried them towards Mr. Lambert's shop. Later, he'd scrub the shells to make sure the clams were ready to be sold and toss any scraps to the cats who regularly visited the fish market. For now, he just needed to soak them in water while he grabbed a bite to eat for himself.

While fishing was hard work, Christopher couldn't have been more grateful for his job with Mr. Lambert. He knew he had made the right decision in choosing to come to Menemsha when Josiah Winslow had so unceremoniously kicked him out of the Winslow barn. As he'd hoped, the fishing village reminded him of home, and the smells of fish and salt water combined with the chattering calls of the village seagulls often made him feel as if he had landed back in Galway. Farming was not for him. He'd always known he belonged on the sea.

Mr. Lambert had given him a room above his shop right after Christopher first arrived in Menemsha. Lambert had been getting ready to take his boat out to fish when he'd seen the young man trudging into the village in the early morning hours before dawn. When Christopher had explained his predicament, Lambert had offered him a room in exchange for help with his fishing business. Christopher had been thrilled to accept.

Now, Christopher had earned enough in wages to be able to start putting some money aside after he paid Mr. Lambert for his room and board. He planned to continue to work and save throughout the upcoming summer and hoped he'd have enough money in his pocket by the fall to once again buy a ticket for Savannah. He wanted to get away from New England before the winter cold returned.

Christopher whistled softly to himself as he walked to the village's general store where he intended to buy a fresh supply of sea biscuits for his lunch. He stopped in his tracks as he saw a woman walking up the wooden steps to the door of the store. While her face was nearly covered by a bonnet, Christopher would have known her petite frame and the auburn hair that escaped her bonnet anywhere. Stella.

He quickened his pace and caught up with her before she could enter the store.

"Mrs. Winslow," he said.

Stella froze as she heard the sound of his voice. She turned around, her face breaking into a broad smile when she saw him.

"Mr. Casey. How good it is to see you."

Christopher bounded up the stairs behind her and held the door open for her. "As it is you, ma'am."

Stella blushed and walked into the store ahead of Christopher.

"How are you?" she asked. "Are you staying here in Menemsha? Do you have a job here?"

"Yes, I am and yes, I do. And, I'm very well, thank you. And you?"

Stella ignored his question. "Who are you working for?"

"Mr. Lambert. I rent a room above his fish market."

"I'm can't say I'm surprised to hear that," Stella said. She grinned and wrinkled her nose. "The smell of fish is all over you."

Christopher grinned. "I don't doubt that. We've been clamming this morning and I just got off the boat not 15 minutes ago." He pointed towards the basket Stella carried in her arms. "What brings you here to the store today?"

"I need flour and sugar," Stella said as she navigated the aisle filled with large barrels of dry cooking ingredients. She pulled canvas sacks from her basket and prepared to fill them.

Christopher grabbed the scoop from the barrel and filled it with flour. "Allow me," he said.

Stella held the bag open. "Thank you."

After filling the bags, Christopher took the now heavy basket from Stella's arm and placed it on his own.

"I can carry that myself you know," Stella said.

"I do know that. But humor me and allow me to carry it for you."

Stella blushed again and her smile widened. "Your arm appears to be healed," she said.

"Mostly. It still aches now and then, but I'm sure that will pass in time."

"And your hand?"

Christopher held up his hand in response. "See for yourself."

Although it was clear Christopher would have a scar for life, the gash was now closed and the wound completely healed.

"You'll have a scar there," Stella said.

"I don't mind. It'll be a reminder of my nurse."

Stella didn't think her face could turn any more red. She hoped Mrs. Poole and the other customers in the store didn't notice. "And what are you here to purchase for yourself, Mr. Casey?"

"Sea biscuits for my lunch. And probably for my dinner too, come to that. They're the cheapest item Mrs. Poole sells here."

"They're not exactly tasty though, are they?"

"They taste alright. I've certainly had worse."

Stella couldn't stop herself from thinking how much she would like to cook for Christopher and fix her mother's recipes for him. She'd lost count of how many times she'd imagined him at her table since Josiah had kicked him out of their home.

The two paid for their respective items, and Christopher carried Stella's basket outside to the store's porch. He gestured at the bench next to the store.

"Do you have time to sit here with me while I eat my biscuits?" Christopher asked. "If you can stand the smell of me, that is."

Stella laughed. "I do have time, yes. And the sea air helps hide your odor."

Christopher laughed in return. "I do believe that's the first time I've ever been told I have an odor. I suppose everyone else has just been polite." He grinned down at Stella. "I thought you had better manners, Mrs. Winslow."

Stella cringed at the name. "Would you call me Stella, please?"

"I'd be honored. If you'll call me Christopher."

"Of course." Stella paused and chewed on her lip. "I'm glad to see you," she said. "I've wanted to apologize to you."

"For what?"

"For my husband's behavior when he forced you to leave our home."

"He was well within his rights. There was no reason for me to continue to impose on your hospitality."

"He had no right to send you away in the dark of night. Before I could even.." Stella shook her head.

"Before you could even what?"

Stella stared up at Christopher. "I wanted to say goodbye to you. He had no right to deprive me of that."

Christopher resisted the urge to reach down and brush away the strand of hair that had fallen into Stella's eyes. "I wanted to say goodbye to you, too," he said.

"It wasn't like Josiah to behave in such a way. He hasn't been himself."

Christopher thought back to his conversation with Mrs. Luce at the apothecary, and his own surprise when Dr. Winslow had sent him to pick up more orders of pain medication on the day he'd asked him to leave the Winslow home.

"Perhaps he hasn't been well," he said.

"If that's so he hasn't shared it with me." Stella shook her head. "He doesn't share anything with me."

Christopher stared out towards the sea and wondered, not for the first time, how Stella had ended up married to Josiah. He'd learned his lesson though and wouldn't ask her again. He looked towards the west and saw the Gay Head light in the distance, its beacon bright even at the height of the afternoon sun.

"I look up there quite often and think of Mr. and Mrs. Mayhew," he said. "And of the men who rowed that boat out to save me. I owe them all so much."

Stella followed his gaze towards the lighthouse. "I haven't seen Mrs. Mayhew since you were rescued. I miss her."

"I've been meaning to walk up there and visit them," Christopher said. "Now that I've got some money in my pocket I want to pay them for their kindness."

"You know they don't expect you to pay them."

"Maybe not, but I expect it of myself."

Stella's mind wandered as she continued to stare at the lighthouse. She imagined visiting Mrs. Mayhew with Christopher. They could walk to the lighthouse together and have dinner with the Mayhews then watch the sun set over the sea from the top of the cliffs.

"Penny for your thoughts," Christopher said.

Stella jumped, startled by the intrusion of his voice into her daydreams. She had nearly forgotten where she was.

"I'll decline that offer, thank you," she said. "I fear if I told you you'd be sure I'm no longer of sane mind."

"I doubt that."

"Are you planning to stay on here in Menemsha?" Stella asked, changing the subject.

"Through the summer, if Mr. Lambert will have me. I hope to be able to leave in the autumn."

"And go where?"

"To Savannah." Christopher smiled. "I still want to go where it's warm."

Stella's heart sank and, to her surprise, she struggled to fight back tears. She cleared her throat and forced a smile onto her face. "I do hope you'll be able to make it this time," she said.

"I hope so, too."

"I thought perhaps after your last sea voyage you might decide to make our island your home."

"It wouldn't be a bad home," Christopher said. "But back in Ireland I always dreamed of going to the warm sunshine. I remember hearing about Florida and thinking it sounded like paradise."

"It gets warm here in the summer, you know," Stella said, unable to stop herself. What was she thinking trying to convince him to stay on the Vineyard? What purpose could it possibly serve?

Christopher laughed. "I'm looking forward to finding that out for myself."

He finished his last bite of biscuit and returned his attention back out to the sea. "I suppose I should be getting back to work now."

Stella jumped from the bench as if she'd been shot. "Of course. And I should be heading home."

"I wish I could walk you back," Christopher said sincerely. "It's a long walk for a lady carrying a heavy basket."

"I've walked it many times," Stella said.

Christopher reached out and touched Stella's shoulder. "Thank you for keeping me company while I ate my lunch," he said.

Stella's heart rate quickened as his hand seemed to burn through her cape and dress. Feeling like a trapped rabbit, she backed away from his touch. "You're welcome. It was my pleasure."

"Good day then," he said, his eyes never leaving Stella's face.

"Good day to you, Christopher."

Christopher reluctantly turned away and headed back towards Mr. Lambert's shop and the piles of clams that were waiting there for him. Stella watched him walk down the narrow dirt road and fought the urge to run after him. She scolded herself and prayed that no one was around to witness her behavior. What would they think of her? And worse, what would Josiah think?

She turned on her heels and headed back down the road towards home. While she tried to force Christopher from her mind, there was one thought she couldn't banish. It propelled her forward and lightened her steps as she walked.

She now knew where Christopher was. And she couldn't wait to return to Menemsha.

****

Stella's heart fluttered with anticipation as she watched her husband hitch Grover up to the buggy and head out to Cottage City to pick up yet another medication order. She couldn't understand why he was ordering so much more than usual, but she knew better than to ask questions about his practice. She noticed him wincing as he climbed into the buggy and was certain he was once again in pain, but whenever she'd asked him if he was feeling poorly he'd denied it and in fact scoffed at her questions. She'd finally given up after her offer to help hitch up the buggy had nearly resulted in Josiah giving her a backhanded slap across the face.

Now she couldn't deny that she cared little about whatever was afflicting Josiah. All that mattered to her was that there was no way he'd return from his trip to Cottage City before evening. Which meant she had plenty of time to walk to Menemsha and back.

Stella hurried into her kitchen and filled a basket with the extra bread and biscuits she had made the night before. Josiah never paid attention to what she cooked as long as he had his own meals. It had been easy to prepare extra baked goods and set them aside in her bread drawer. She added a chunk of cheese from her ice chest and closed the basket.

Stella tied her bonnet under her chin and tossed her cape over her shoulders. She didn't think she really needed the cape since the spring had been unseasonably warm, but decided it was better to be safe than sorry. As she walked towards the road, she heard Henry running behind her. The dog gently nudged the back of her legs, as if he was reminding her that she had forgotten him.

"You stay home, Henry," Stella said, ruffling the dog's furry head. "I'll be back soon."

Henry barked and continued to follow her. Stella stopped walking and pointed towards the porch.

"Henry, go home."

The dog wiggled and ignored her command. He ran ahead of her and stopped on the road and looked back at her as if he was waiting for her to catch up.

Stella couldn't help but laugh. "So you won't do as you're told?"

Henry barked and wagged his tail in response.

"Alright, you silly dog. You can come with me."

Stella reached the road and walked briskly in the direction of Menemsha with Henry running along at her side.

"Do you want to see Christopher, Henry?"

Stella laughed as the dog cocked his ears as if trying to understand her question.

"Mr. Casey," she said. "You remember him, don't you?"

Henry barked again and ran ahead of Stella on the road. Stella's pulse quickened as they came to Mememsha creek and she could see the village in the distance. She hoped Christopher would be taking his lunch at the usual time.

She soon saw him standing on the dock talking to Mr. Lambert as they hauled the morning's catch from the Lambert boat. Christopher was hard to miss in his yellow oil-cloth fishing jacket and pants. Stella watched as he slipped out of his outerwear and left the clothing in a pile on the dock. She smiled as he walked off the dock and headed for the general store. Stella stepped up her pace and urged Henry to do the same.

"Christopher," she called out.

He turned to her and smiled. "Stella. Good day to you." Henry ran to Christopher and jumped at his legs. "And Henry," he said, scratching the dog's ears. "How are you, boy?"

Stella gestured towards Christopher with her basket. "I brought you some lunch. And some extra food for dinner, too."

"So I can skip sea biscuits for today?" Christopher asked, continuing to pet the wiggling dog.

"And for tomorrow as well, if you eat wisely."

Stella reached Christopher and let out a deep breath as she looked up into his smiling face. His brown curls were as out of control as always, and he now had a growth of dark stubble on his cheeks and chin to match his hair. She had come to enjoy her meetings with him so much that she'd even learned to ignore the stench of fish that clung to him.

They sat down on the bench that Stella now considered their own, and Christopher hungrily removed the food she had brought him from the basket. Henry begged for a handout but quickly settled on the ground at Stella's feet once she shot him a stern reprimand. Stella removed her cape and soaked up the spring sunshine. She couldn't remember when she'd felt more content.

"Your eyes are beautiful when the sun hits them like that," Christopher said.

Stella turned the familiar shade of red that always accompanied her meetings with Christopher. "Thank you," she said. "It's a beautiful day, isn't it?"

"Perfect," Christopher said, his gaze never wavering from her face.

"Did you and Mr. Lambert have a good catch this morning?"

"We did. There are plenty of clams and scallops waiting for me this afternoon."

"I wish I could stay here and help you."

"You wouldn't say that if you'd done the work. It's difficult."

"I know all about hard work," Stella said. "I have my own waiting for me at home." Stella shuddered as she thought about the basket of laundry and the pile of sewing that needed to be completed. She had to be careful to make sure most of her work was done when Josiah got home so he wouldn't ask any questions. Stella rubbed Henry's back with her foot. "Though at least I have Henry to keep me company."

"I have company as well," Christopher said, pointing to a group of cats who were prowling the dock. "See those cats? They come to Mr. Lambert's every day waiting for the spoiled fish we toss out. The big black one is my favorite. I call him Cian."

"Is that an Irish name?"

Christopher nodded. "It means ancient. That cat is an old soul, I think. I can see it in his eyes."

Stella grasped the bench with her hands and swung her feet back and forth in front of her. "We have cats around the barn," she said. "They come and go, but they keep the rats away for us."

"I'm very familiar with your barn cats. I made their acquaintance when we shared our sleeping quarters."

Stella frowned. "I'm still ashamed of that. Josiah was wrong to make you sleep in the barn when we have perfectly good rooms in the house."

"It was fine with me. Like I said then, I've slept in much worse places."

Christopher thought back to the day Stella had invited him to stay at the Winslow home, remembering Josiah's words and the spare rooms for the children he expected to have.

"Dr. Winslow made a comment about children and the rooms in your house, as I recall," he said. "It upset you."

"His goal was to upset me."

"What did he mean by that remark?"

Stella glanced up at Christopher and shook her head. "I shouldn't talk about such things with you."

"I apologize if I've been too forward." He took a bite of cheese and followed it with some of Stella's bread. "The food is wonderful. Thank you."

"You're welcome. I can't have you eating those biscuits every day."

Stella stared out at the harbor and watched as more fishing boats returned from their morning trips.

"I haven't been able to give Josiah any children," she said quietly. "I've lost them all."

"I'm sorry."

"He resents me for it, I know. He wants a son so badly."

Christopher put down his food and followed Stella's gaze out to the sea. He felt awkward and had no idea what to say, and silently cursed himself for bringing up such a delicate and uncomfortable subject.

"His first wife was with child when she died," Stella said.

"What happened to her? Did she die of consumption like your parents?"

"No, she died in childbirth actually. Neither she nor the baby survived." Stella paused and let out a breath. "Josiah was devastated, I know. He loved her."

Christopher felt the pain in the words she left unspoken. Her husband didn't love her.

"He was different back then," Stella continued. "He was a friend of my father's and he and his wife Lillian visited our house quite often. When my parents died I had no one."

"So that's how you ended up married to him," Christopher said softly.

Stella turned to face him. "Josiah wanted another wife after Lillian died. And he wanted to expand his practice. My parents' land was very valuable..."

Christopher met her gaze. "That's not a very romantic story."

Stella scoffed. "It's life though, isn't it? There's nothing about life that's very romantic."

Christopher thought back to the loss of his mother, when he'd found himself alone and penniless in a country fraught with turmoil.

"No, there's not."

Henry rolled onto his side and offered his belly to Stella. She smiled and continued to rub him with her foot. For the briefest of moments, she thought how romantic life actually would be if she could stay here with Christopher like this forever.

"You two here again?"

A woman's voice from behind them caused both Christopher and Stella to jump. They turned and saw the shopkeeper Mrs. Poole staring at them, her hands on her ample hips. Both leaped to their feet.

"Mrs. Poole, hello," Stella said. She lifted her basket from the bench. "I've just come to buy some more flour from you."

The other woman eyed her quizzically. "You do go through a lot of flour these days, Stella."

"Doing a great deal of baking," Stella said. "I think it's the spring weather. It brings me such energy."

Mrs. Poole nodded, clearly unconvinced. "No biscuits for you today, Mr. Casey?"

"Not today, ma'am," Christopher said. "Mrs. Winslow was kind enough to share her lunch with me." He knew there was no point in lying. The food was on the bench for anyone to see.

Including Henry, who saw Mrs. Poole's arrival as an opportunity to steal the block of cheese Christopher had left with his bread. Stella caught him and pushed him from the bench, secretly glad the dog had given her an excuse to look away from the accusing eyes of the shopkeeper.

"Henry, you behave," she said, sitting back down on the bench and turning her back on Mrs. Poole.

The shopkeeper snorted and turned back towards her store.

"Good day to you, Mrs. Poole," Christopher said.

"And to you, Mr. Casey."

To Christopher's immense relief, the woman disappeared inside the store. He sat back down on the bench and quickly packed up his bread and cheese in the towels Stella had provided for him.

"I suppose I need to be getting back to work now," he said.

Stella tried to keep her hands from shaking as she smoothed the fur on Henry's head. "I was wrong to come here and visit you. I should have known better."

"No, it's fine," Christopher said.

"You don't know the way people are here. They love to talk." Stella thought back to the night Josiah had pinned her to the wall. "I should have thought of this before. This was a terrible mistake. Josiah will find out..."

"Find out what? That you had lunch with a friend? We haven't done anything wrong."

"That's not what Mrs. Poole thinks."

"Who cares what she thinks?" Christopher said. "I never met a nastier woman. She's a sour old hag, that one is.

Stella stood up and threw her cape over her shoulders. "I should have known better," she repeated.

Christopher grabbed her shaking hands in his own. "You've done nothing wrong."

Stella pulled her hands away and shook her head. "I shan't come here again," she said. "I'm sorry."

Christopher stood helpless as she turned away and nearly ran from him, beckoning Henry to follow her. He watched as their figures grew smaller on the road and finally turned away as the ends of Stella's cape fluttered out of his sight. As he started to head back to Mr. Lambert's, he nearly tripped over a warm body rubbing along his legs. Looking down, he saw a large and familiar coal black cat.

"Hello, Cian," he said. "You wanting some cheese now, are you?"

He opened his bundle of food and broke off a piece of cheese for the cat.

"That's all you're getting," he said. "I dare say I won't have any more any time soon."

Christopher took one look back towards the Chilmark road and, for a brief moment, he longed to run after Stella and follow her. He shook his head at his own silliness and turned instead towards Mr. Lambert's shop. Cian followed behind.

****

Josiah finished his supper and stood up from the table, pushing his chair back and causing the legs to screech against the floor.

"When Mrs. Poole arrives," he said, "show her to my office."

Stella's dinner plate slipped from her hands and shattered into chunks on the floor.

Josiah jumped at the noise. "Lord, woman, what's the matter with ya?"

"I'm sorry," Stella said as she bent over to pick up the plate and tried to keep her hands from shaking. "Just clumsy."

"I reckon so."

"What did you say about Mrs. Poole, Josiah?"

"I said when she arrives show her to my office."

"Why is she coming here?"

"She's here to purchase some medication for Mr. Poole. I saw her at the apothecary yesterday and she told me he slipped down the stairs and hurt his ankle something terrible. I told her I'd come have a look at him, but she said that wouldn't be necessary. Just needs something to get him through the pain of it."

"Poor Mr. Poole. I do hope he's alright."

"Are you done with your questions now? I have work to do."

Stella tossed the broken pieces of plate into the trash and finished clearing the table. "Of course."

Her hands trembled as she put the dishes into the pail of hot soapy water. Of all the people who could be coming to her home, Mrs. Poole was literally the last person she wanted to see. She had convinced herself that she had overreacted about their encounter in Menemsha. She had stayed away from the village and from Christopher for a few weeks now, and she was certain the whole incident was behind her. As soon as she'd heard the shopkeeper's name that certainty had vanished.

She jumped and nearly dropped another dish when she heard a knock at her front door. Stella dried her hands on her apron and walked to the doorway. She forced her face into a smile as she opened it.

"Good day to you, Mrs. Poole," she said.

"And to you, Stella."

"My husband is expecting you. He asked that I show you to his office."

The shopkeeper nodded and walked into Stella's living room.

"I was sorry to hear about Mr. Poole's accident."

"Thank you."

"Please give him my best."

"Will do."

Stella couldn't help but notice that the other woman never once met her eyes. And her face never showed even the slightest hint of a smile.

She brushed past the woman and led her to Josiah's office. She knocked on the closed door.

"Mrs. Poole is here for you, Josiah."

"Send her in," Josiah called.

Stella opened the door and nodded to Mrs. Poole as she stepped inside the office. Josiah rose from his chair and shut the door without another word to Stella.

She stood outside the door for a few minutes, desperately trying to hear what was being said inside. She could only pick up bits and pieces, as both Mrs. Poole and her husband were talking quietly. From what she could hear, they were only talking about Mr. Poole's fall and resulting injury.

Stella shook her head at her own foolishness. She was letting fear get the better of her. There was work to be done before nightfall and she shouldn't be wasting time eavesdropping on her husband. If he opened the door and found her this way she'd never be able to explain her behavior.

Scolding herself, she went back to the kitchen and finished cleaning up before heading outside to feed her sheep and to brush and groom Grover. She brought along some carrots she had saved for Grover while preparing dinner and stuffed them into the pocket of her dress. As always, her animals made her smile, and she quickly forgot about her worries over Mrs. Poole's visit.

The sun was nearly set when Mrs. Poole and Josiah emerged from the house. Stella sat on a bale of hay in the barn and brushed the mats from Henry's fur as she watched her husband escort Mrs. Poole to her waiting buggy and driver. Stella's fear had returned while she waited for Mrs. Poole to leave her home, and her anxiety now increased with each minute that passed.

Josiah held Mrs. Poole's hand as she climbed into the back of her buggy, and Stella was sure she saw him grimace in pain as he bore the brunt of the shopkeeper's weight. He showed only smiles to Mrs. Poole though and waved as she and her driver drove off down the road. Stella's hand froze in Henry's fur as her husband turned around to face the barn. Even in the rapidly darkening evening, Stella could see the contempt on his face as his eyes met hers.

Sure he was headed for the barn, she braced herself for a confrontation. But instead of walking towards her, Josiah turned instead for the front door and walked briskly inside. Stella got up from the hay and said a quick goodnight to the animals before heading back into her kitchen.

She took a deep breath as she went indoors and tried to prepare herself for what she was sure would be an angry tirade from Josiah. But to her surprise, he was nowhere to be found. She walked to his office and found his door closed and the light from the oil lamp glowing underneath the door.

Stella tip-toed away from the office and headed for the bedroom she shared with her husband. Perhaps her nerves had gotten the better of her and she had merely imagined the look on Josiah's face. Surely he wouldn't let the issue go if Mrs. Poole had indeed told him about Stella's meetings with Christopher.

She quietly changed into her dressing gown and gratefully slipped into her empty bed. With luck, Josiah would not wake her when he decided to retire himself. She tried again to convince herself that his apparent anger when Mrs. Poole had left had simply been a product of her imagination.

But no matter how hard she tried to believe it, she knew what she had seen when Josiah had looked at her. And she knew she had seen anger. More than that, she was sure she had seen hatred.

****

Two days passed before Stella knew she was right about what she had seen. Josiah barely spoke to her, but he treated her cordially and in the business-like manner normally reserved for strangers. He never once met her gaze and, to her relief, never touched her in their bed. In fact, he never touched her at all. The tension in their home grew with each passing hour.

And then exploded on the afternoon of the third day, when Josiah returned from visiting patients. He ignored her when she came outside to unhitch Grover and feed him, brushing past her and going into the house without a word. When she finished with the horse and came inside, he was waiting for her in the kitchen.

Stella stopped short, startled at the way her husband was staring at her, his face a hideous mask of unsuppressed fury.

"Josiah?" she asked. "Is something wrong?"

Without a word, Josiah strode across the kitchen and slapped her across the face.

Stella gasped in pain, and tears instantly sprung from her eyes. She cradled her burning cheek in her hand and stared up at her husband. Before she could speak, he slapped her again, this time across her other cheek.

"You want to know if something is wrong?" he asked. "Does that give you an answer?"

Stella backed away from him, pinning herself into the corner of the kitchen. He followed and towered over her, glaring down at her with a rage that made her tremble with fear.

"Josiah," she said, her voice choked with sobs. "What..."

He smacked her again before she could finish her question.

"Be quiet!" he yelled.

Stella screamed as he grabbed her arm and twisted it around her back as he leaned into her.

"You don't think I know what you've been doing?" Josiah asked, his breath hot and foul against her face. "Parading around the island like some sort of strumpet?"

"Josiah, please..."

"I said be quiet! You shan't insult me by pretending you don't know what I'm speaking of."

Stella let out a squeal of pain as he twisted her arm again.

"Mrs. Poole told me all about your trips to Menemsha," he said. "Told me how you've been meeting that God-forsaken mick behind my back. Did I not warn you about making a fool of me?"

"I haven't. Please..."

"Shut your bone box, woman! I went to Menemsha this morning," Josiah said, spitting out the words as if they were poison in his mouth. "Your mucker was out on the boat with Lambert but I talked to some of the village folks. I heard all about your visits there. Bringing that boy food and giggling at him like some godless hussy. I won't have it, Stella, do you understand me?" He twisted her arm again until Stella let out a cry of pain. "I won't have it!"

Josiah let her go and tossed her to the kitchen floor. To Stella's surprise, he doubled over and clutched his stomach in pain. She stared at him, afraid to speak. Josiah recovered himself and stood straight again, towering over her as she cowered on the floor.

"Get up," he said.

Stella shook her head. "Please, Josiah..."

He grabbed her arm again. "I said get up!"

Josiah pulled Stella to her feet and shoved her against the wall. "You'll pay for this, Stella," he said. "You and that boy both. You'll pay for this."

Stella let out a sob, unable to speak.

"What would your father think of you?" Josiah said. "His own daughter. No better than a two-bit strumpet making a fool of herself in front of his neighbors. With a mick, of all things."

"He's my friend," Stella said. "That's all."

"Only thing worse than a cheating hussy is a lying one."

Stella flinched as Josiah raised his hand once again. She braced herself for the sting of his slap, but heard a knock at their door instead. Josiah lowered his hand and gave her a smile that chilled her to her core.

"I told you you'd pay for this, didn't I?"

He chuckled and strode towards the front door, leaving Stella shaking and crying in the kitchen. She heard Josiah speaking to their visitor, but she couldn't make out who it was. And she dared not leave the kitchen until she could stop trembling and control her tears.

To her surprise, she heard the door shut and Josiah leave the house with his guest. She heard voices coming from the field and quickly ran to the kitchen door. She saw Josiah walking with their neighbor Thomas West, the man who had bought her father's land and sheep. And what she saw next made her stomach retch. Josiah and West entered the barn and quickly came back outside with the sheep in tow. Stella ran outside and into the field.

"What's happening?" she said. "What are you doing with my sheep?"

"Not your sheep, my dear," Josiah said. "They belong to Mr. West now."

Stella looked back and forth between Thomas West and her husband, no longer caring if her neighbor saw her red and tear-stained face. "What do you mean?" she asked. "Of course they belong to me. What are you doing?"

"I'm not doing anything. It's all been done. I sold the sheep to Mr. West this afternoon."

"You can't mean this, Josiah."

"Stella, get back in the house. You look as if you've had some sort of fit. I'll be finished with Mr. West here shortly and then I'll join you. I know you have dinner to prepare."

Stella ignored him and gasped in horror as Mr. West started to rope her sheep and bring them to his wagon.

"You can't take my sheep," she said, running towards him.

"I've bought the sheep, Mrs. Winslow," West said, obviously confused. "The doctor here told me you couldn't keep up with caring for them anymore."

"That's a lie," Stella yelled.

Josiah grasped her arm and held it with a steel grip.

"Stella," he said. "You're making a fool of yourself. Go inside and get yourself together."

He turned towards Mr. West. "I think you can see now why I told you before that my dear wife hasn't been well. She's not herself."

West nodded and looked at Stella with pity as he herded the sheep to his wagon and tied them to the back.

"Don't forget the dog," Josiah said.

"What?" Stella cried out. "What dog?"

"Henry!" Josiah called. "Come here, boy."

Stella screamed as Henry ran out from the barn. "No, Josiah, please. I beg you, no!"

"A sheep herding dog belongs with sheep, my dear. You know that perfectly well." Josiah tightened his grip on her arm.

Stella grew dizzy as she watched Mr. West put a rope around Henry's neck and place him on the front seat of his wagon. She collapsed at her husband's feet as the neighbor got into the wagon beside the dog who looked from Josiah to his new owner with fear and confusion.

"Please don't take my dog," Stella cried. "Please."

Josiah sighed. "Go along now, Mr. West," he said. "It's the vapors, like I told you. She'll be okay once she gets some rest. I do apologize for this unfortunate scene."

Stella sobbed on the ground as the wagon disappeared up the road, her sheep in tow. She gasped in pain and fright as Josiah grabbed her arm again and pulled her towards the house.

She stumbled inside behind him with no time to catch her breath before he closed the door and threw her against it.

"I told you you'd pay, didn't I?" he said, grinning.

"How could you?" Stella said. "I hate you, you know that? I hate you!"

Josiah clenched his fist and punched her as hard as he could in the face, knocking her to the floor.

Stella cried out as he kicked her stomach. She curled into a ball, desperate to protect herself from her husband's rage. She screamed when he pulled her to her feet and trapped her against the wall.

"I'm not finished yet, Stella," he hissed. "You'll see."

He opened the door and threw Stella onto the porch.

"I want you out now, you hear me? I won't have strumpets in my home."

"It's my home," Stella cried. "It's always been my home."

Josiah kicked her again, striking her thigh with the hard toe of his boot. "Be gone, Stella," he yelled. "I shan't look at your filthy face again."

Josiah slammed the door, leaving Stella curled into a ball on their porch. The sun had disappeared below the horizon now, and darkness had set in over the farm.

Stella pulled herself to her feet and clutched her abdomen in pain. She wondered if Josiah's kick had broken a rib. She felt dizzy and disoriented, and her face throbbed where he had punched her. She touched her eye, finding it half-closed from swelling.

She stumbled away from the house without looking back. She knew Josiah would be watching her through the window and she didn't want him to have the satisfaction of seeing her beg for re-entry into the home she had lived in all of her life.

She got to the road and quickly made a decision which way to turn. She knew where she was going. She had nowhere else to go.

****

Stella stumbled and tripped over a tree root as she tried to navigate her way in the darkness of the island night. Tiny pebbles tore through her thin dress and scraped her knee. She felt warm trickles of blood as she put her hand to her knee. Compared to the pain she felt on her face, abdomen, and leg, the knee was minor and nothing but a nuisance at this point.

She had to ignore all of it and focus on her goal, which was to find Christopher at Menemsha. He'd help her; she had no doubt of that. If she let her brain process what had happened back at home she knew she wouldn't be able to keep going. She had to block out not only the physical but also the emotional anguish Josiah's cruelty had caused her.

Stella was grateful for the stars and the clear full moon that gave her some light in the midnight sky. She followed the stars towards the sea and eventually came to Memensha Creek. While she couldn't see the village well enough to make out the buildings, she knew exactly where Mr. Lambert's shop was. She could find her way there using the light of the stars and the sounds of the buoys in the harbor as her guides.

Feeling overwhelmed with relief when she finally came to Mr. Lambert's shop, Stella tripped up the wooden stairs and fell once again, this time landing on the Lambert porch. Trembling, she picked herself up and slipped inside the shop, praying she wouldn't wake the fisherman from his sleep. She was relieved to hear snoring coming from the room at the back of the shop, and felt safe that Mr. Lambert was indeed sleeping soundly.

Stella knew that Christopher was staying above the shop, and her eyes scanned the room for a ladder or a staircase. She was once again grateful for the stars and the full moon, as their light shone through the window and illuminated a ladder that extended up to a loft above the store.

Moving as quietly as her feet would allow, Stella climbed up the ladder and peered into the darkness of the loft.

"Christopher?" she whispered.

There was no response. Stella pulled herself into the loft and sat down on the floor. She didn't want to risk knocking into any furniture or supplies and making enough noise to wake up Mr. Lambert.

"Christopher?"

Stella could hear the heavy breathing of deep sleep and she was sure she heard Christopher. She inched forward on her hands and knees towards the breathing sounds.

She stopped when she came to Christopher's bed, which was nothing but a mattress on the floor of the loft. She wanted to touch him but didn't want to frighten him and cause him to yell out.

"Christopher," she said again. "Christopher, please wake up."

Christopher stirred on the bed, and Stella longed to be able to see him. But the loft was pitch black.

She gently reached out and touched what she thought would be Christopher's shoulder. "Christopher, it's Stella. Please, I need you to wake up."

Christopher sat up with a start, causing Stella to jump and nearly fall backwards down the ladder.

"Who's there?" Christopher asked.

"Stella. I need help." Stella couldn't stop the flow of tears down her swollen cheeks. "Please help me."

"Stella! What in God's name?"

"Shh. We can't wake Mr. Lambert."

Christopher rubbed his eyes and tried to shake the sleep from his head.

"What are you doing here?" he whispered. "What's happened?"

"Josiah banished me from our home. And not just that. He beat me." Stella burst into tears. "He kicked me and punched me in the face."

"He did what?" Christopher's voice rose and the two both froze as they heard Mr. Lambert's bed creaking downstairs.

Christopher let out a deep breath and returned his voice to a whisper. "Josiah did what to you?" he repeated.

"He beat me."

Christopher fumbled around next to his mattress and found the lantern he used to light the loft each evening. He lit it and held it up near Stella's face. What he saw sent rivers of rage coursing through his body.

Her eye was swollen to little more than a slit, and the skin surrounding it was a bright shade of purple and green. Her cheeks were flaming red and blood trickled from her nose. Her top lip was split and swollen to twice its normal size.

"Jesus, Mary, and Joseph," he said.

"It was Mrs. Poole," Stella said. "She came to his office for medication and she told him about our lunches. He went crazy, Christopher. He's gone mad."

"He's worse than mad. What kind of man could do this to you?"

"He believes I've been unfaithful to him with you." Stella collapsed into tears and buried her face in her hands. "I don't know what to do, Christopher. I don't know what I'm going to do."

Christopher wrapped his arms around Stella and pulled her to his chest. "Hush now," he whispered. "You'll be alright, Aingilín. You'll be alright."

Christopher kissed Stella's head and rocked her gently until her sobs quieted. He gently lifted her head to his face and kissed her swollen lips.

"We can't stay here," he said. "Mr. Lambert will be up soon and getting ready to go out for the morning. But I know a place I can take you where you'll be safe until we figure out what to do."

Stella nodded. "Take me there, please."

"I just need to get my wages from downstairs. Mr. Lambert's kept the money I've saved in his safe for me. But we'll need it now, wherever we end up." Christopher sighed. "I hate to think of Mr. Lambert waking up and wandering where I've disappeared to when he heads out on the boat. Once we get you safe, I'll have to beg for his forgiveness."

"I'm sorry for involving you in this."

Christopher kissed the top of her head. "Hush with that silliness, lass. You've nothing to apologize for and you didn't involve me in anything."

He disappeared down the ladder with his lantern, and Stella sat as still as she could and prayed he wouldn't wake his employer. She needed to get to the safe place Christopher promised her and didn't think she could handle a setback of any sort. Now that she had reached Christopher, her single-minded determination in making her trek to Menemsha had deserted her and she was overwhelmed by the pain that wracked her body. She was now so exhausted that she feared she may simply collapse.

Stella nearly cried again as Christopher returned with the lantern.

"Mr. Lambert didn't wake up, did he?"

Christopher shook his head. "No. Thanks be to God he's a sound sleeper."

Christopher quickly pulled his clothes on over the undergarments he slept in and helped Stella get up from the mattress. He grabbed a sack he kept next to his bed and put his coat over her trembling shoulders.

"Where's your cloak?" he asked.

"He didn't let me take it. He just kicked me out the door and left me on the porch."

Christopher swallowed his rage and picked up his gloves from the small stand next to his mattress. "You can wear these as well."

"You'll need them."

"I'm fine." He smiled and kissed Stella's nose as she stood before him. "It's my turn to take care of you, yeah?"

Christopher took Stella's gloved hand and led her down the ladder to the first floor of Mr. Lambert's shop. He had blown out the lantern before they descended and now moved with the grace of a cat through the pitch black room. Leading Stella back out onto the porch of the shop, he closed the door behind them without making a sound.

Christopher stopped and re-lit the lantern, illuminating the road ahead of them and giving them a clear path through the village. Taking Stella by the hand, he walked quickly towards the docks where Mr. Lambert kept his boat. Stella could see the fishing boats bobbing in the water under the glow of the full moon.

"There's an abandoned boat shack close by," Christopher said. "Mr. Lambert told me the owner left the island for the winter and isn't to return until summer. He warned the fisherman here to leave it be while he was gone. Apparently he's a fierce fellow, because they've all listened."

Christopher held up his lantern and pointed towards a small ramshackle house on the edge of the docks. Two rectangles of wood which Stella imagined had once been doors hung haphazardly from rusted hinges.

"There aren't any doors here," she said.

"It doesn't matter. Who do you think is around to see us? And besides, as long as we stay over at the other side of the shack we'll be hidden by the boat anyway."

Skeptical, Stella followed Christopher into the shack and looked around at the ropes and buckets that dotted the floor. A small fishing boat had been towed into the shack, and an assortment of tarps and fishing lines stuck haphazardly out of it.

"Come here," Christopher said, leading Stella to the corner wall of the shack. "No one can see us over here even if they do happen to glance in."

He sat down on the floor of the shack and pulled Stella down next to him. Christopher put his arm around her shoulder as she rested her head against his chest.

"You can rest now," he whispered

"Do you need your coat?" Stella asked. "You'll be cold."

"I have you to keep me warm," Christopher said. "But I wouldn't mind if you turned yourself into a blanket."

Stella smiled against his chest. She climbed onto Christopher's lap and wrapped her arms around his torso.

"How's that suit you?" she asked.

"Perfect. I'm warm as toast."

Christopher kissed the top of Stella's head and smoothed her hair with his hand. "Rest now, Aingilín."

"What's that mean?"

"Little angel."

"I'm not little, you know. I'm a grown woman."

"That I do know. But you're little to me." He took her small hand in his own and kissed her fingers one by one. "You're so tiny."

"Thank you for helping me."

"It's the least I can do for my nurse."

Christopher leaned back against the wall and stared out at Menemsha harbor through what had once been the door of the shack. It was high tide, and Christopher could hear the waves of Vineyard Sound lapping over the jetties that lined the channel separating Menemsha from neighboring Lobsterville. He knew Mr. Lambert would be navigating that channel out to sea in just a few short hours for his day's work. He hoped he would at least get a good catch in spite of the fact that Christopher would not be able to help him with it.

"What are you looking at?"

Christopher jumped, startled at the sound of Stella's voice. "I thought you'd fallen asleep, love."

"I'm not sleeping."

"Then look out there with me, why don't you. It's beautiful, isn't it?"

Stella lifted her head and followed Christopher's gaze out to the harbor surrounding them. The full moon cast a white glow over the water, which was now as dark as the night sky around it.

"I like to sit out on those rocks," Christopher said. "All the way at the very end."

"Why?"

"Because it's peaceful out there. I sit there and sometimes I think if I look really hard, I can see home."

Stella smiled. "You mean Ireland?"

"I do." Christopher pulled Stella up until her cheek rested against his and whispered in her ear as he pointed out at the horizon beyond the rocks. "Look out there. Can't you see it?"

"I think I can, yes."

"That's the Galway harbor. It's the only harbor I've ever seen that's as beautiful as this one is."

"I'd like to go there."

Christopher shook his head. "I don't think you would, love. There are a lot of problems there."

"There are problems everywhere."

"Well trust me when I say you wouldn't enjoy the voyage across the Atlantic."

"It sounds like an adventure to me. I've never been anywhere."

"It's not an adventure I'd recommend."

Stella let out a breath as she settled her head back on Christopher's chest.

"You know what I do when I'm out at the end of those rocks?" he asked.

"No. What do you do?"

"I shout out to those people over in Galway so loud I'm certain they can hear me."

Stella smiled against his chest. "And what exactly do you shout to them, Mr. Casey?"

"That I came here to America and found the most beautiful girl I've ever seen." He kissed Stella's head. "The most beautiful girl in the whole world."

"Is that me you found then?"

"Who else would it be?"

Stella felt a tear roll down her bruised cheek.

"I dare say no one would find me beautiful now."

Christopher lifted her face to his with gentle fingers. He brushed his lips against her swollen eye. "You're beautiful to me."

Stella's face crumpled as her single tear gave way to sobs.

"Oh Christopher," she said. "What's going to happen to me?"

Christopher held her to his chest and brushed her hair with his hand. "Hush, now. You're going to be alright, I promise you that. Please try not to cry," he whispered. "You'll only make your pain worse."

And I can't bear to hear the crying, he thought. Christopher wanted to do nothing so much as go to the Winslow home and give Josiah Winslow the same beating he had given his defenseless wife. But he knew that would only get him in trouble himself. And it would do nothing to help Stella now.

Christopher rested his head against the wall of the shack and closed his eyes. He held Stella close until her sobs quieted and he could feel her steady breathing against his chest. To his relief, she finally drifted off to sleep.

He felt his rage returning and forced himself to swallow it down. Josiah Winslow would answer for what he had done to Stella someday. For now, all that mattered was that Christopher take care of Stella and get her somewhere safe.

He didn't want to admit it to himself, but he had no idea how he was going to do that.

****

Christopher opened his eyes with a start. He briefly wondered where he was, but a glance down at Stella's head on his chest brought the previous night back very quickly. He could see the morning sun shining through the fishing shack and hear the sounds of the village waking up and getting to work. He knew by now Mr. Lambert would have discovered he was gone, and he felt a rush of guilt that he had let his employer down. But he'd had no choice, and he hoped Mr. Lambert would eventually understand that.

He heard a whimper as Stella shifted her body and raised her head from his chest.

"Are you alright, lass?" he whispered.

"No," Stella mumbled. "I can't bear the pain. It hurts everywhere."

Christopher gently raised Stella's head and looked at her face in the morning sun. If possible, it was even more swollen than it had been the night before and her bruises had deepened, casting a rainbow of yellow, purple, and green across her cheek. Christopher felt sure that Josiah had broken a bone in his wife's face when he'd so viciously punched her. In addition, her cracked lip was now dripping blood, and her swollen eye had completely closed. Christopher felt the previous night's rage returning to a boil inside him.

"That God-forsaken bastard," he muttered.

Christopher pulled a handkerchief from the pocket of his trousers and gently blotted the blood from Stella's cracked lip. Unable to stop himself, he kissed her swollen and tear-stained face before closing his eyes and moving his lips to her own. She shifted her weight, sitting up to answer his kiss, and parted her lips to welcome his tongue. Christopher's breath quickened as his fingers slipped from her face to the curve of her breast. His hand traveled the length of her body and lightly touched the bare skin of her leg under her dress. He wrapped his arm around Stella's waist and pulled her body closer to his own. Stella let out a whimper of pain and pulled back.

Christopher opened his eyes. "What is it? Did I hurt you?"

"A little." Stella clutched her stomach. "I think Josiah broke my ribs when he kicked me. I'm sorry."

"Nothing to be sorry for. I'm the one to apologize. I know you're injured."

"I'm sorry," Stella said again.

Christopher kissed the top of her head. "Please don't apologize, love. You're in pain and I'm a selfish bastard."

Stella's mouth curved into as much of a smile as she could manage with her swollen lip. Her finger traced the line of Christopher's jaw. "You're not that. Not at all."

"I am." He smiled and kissed the tip of her nose. "But I do have a defense. I'm mad about you, lass, it's as simple as that. I'm off my chump. Have been since the day I first laid eyes on ye."

"I dare say I'm mad about you, too." Stella said. "Josiah was right about that, at least."

Christopher kissed her again and looked around the shack that had become their sanctuary. "We need to get out of here anyway and get you somewhere safe," he said. He reached for the sack he had grabbed from his living quarters and pulled out a wrapped biscuit. "But first, you need to get some food in you."

"I can't eat now," Stella said.

"Just a few bites." Christopher broke the biscuit into tiny pieces. "You need some nourishment."

Stella nibbled at the pieces of biscuit, each chew bringing a fresh wave of pain to her face. She handed the rest back to Christopher. "That's enough. I can't eat more."

Christopher nodded and quickly scarfed down the remains of the biscuit for his own breakfast. He took a canteen from his sack, grateful that he had filled it the night before when he thought he would be taking it out on the boat in the morning.

"Take a sip of water," he said.

She gratefully took the water and swallowed several gulps before handing the canteen back to Christopher.

"Thank you," she said.

Christopher took a drink himself and wiped his mouth with his sleeve. "We need to get you away from here," he said. "You're not safe on this island with Josiah."

Stella felt a lump in her throat as she realized the enormity of his words. "This island is my home," she said.

"He won't leave you in peace, Stella."

"He's already taken everything from me," Stella said. Tears sprung to her eyes as the events of the previous day returned to the forefront of her mind. "He sold my sheep. And he took Henry away too."

Christopher gritted his teeth. "I'm sorry," he whispered.

Stella shook her head. "I shouldn't have said anything. I can't bear to think of it." She looked straight into his eyes with the one eye she could still open. "Do you have an idea of where I can go then?"

"I do." Christopher reached for his sack and raised it. "I told you last night, I've got this money I've been able to put away. It'll get us on a steamer back to the mainland. I'll find work in New Bedford on the docks."

"You don't want to go to New Bedford, you told me so. You're saving your money for Savannah."

"I was," Christopher said. "Things have changed. I don't have time to save any more money. We need to leave here now."

Stella stared out through the window of the shack and let out a deep breath. She turned back to Christopher. "No. I won't have you taking care of me."

Christopher took her hand. "Stella, that's not how it would be."

"It is. I've already had one man taking care of me and look where it's left me. I shan't have another."

"I wouldn't turn into Josiah on you."

Stella ran a finger along the rough stubble of his cheek. "I didn't mean to imply that you would. But I can't let you give up your plans for me. You'd come to resent me, just like Josiah did."

Christopher shook his head. "I wouldn't."

Stella leaned back next to Christopher along the wall of the shack. "I have my own money," she said. "A great deal of money."

"How's that?"

"The money Josiah got for selling my father's land should be mine. He still has some of it left, and I know where it is."

"You shouldn't go back to that house."

Stella sat up again and looked at him. "I shouldn't go back to my house? It's mine, not Josiah's. It's always been mine."

"That's not the case since you married him. You know that. Everything of yours belongs to him."

Stella fought back tears of anger. "Then I'll take my money and leave him to his house," she said, spitting out the words.

"How can you do that?"

"Josiah will be going out for his appointments today like he always does. I'll simply watch the house from the trees and wait until he leaves. Then I'll slip in and take my money from my father's safe." She turned back to Christopher. "You can come with me. As soon as I have the money we'll leave this place. And we'll use my money to get us both to Savannah."

Christopher shook his head. "I don't know, Stella. I don't think it's safe for you to go near him again."

"I won't be near him. He won't know I've been there until I'm long gone. We'll go to Cottage City and get on the first steamer we find."

Stella felt a rush of excitement as she talked. Now that she had a plan, she couldn't wait to leave this island and her husband behind.

She stood up with difficulty and forced herself to ignore the pain from Josiah's kicks to her stomach and leg. She reached her hand out to Christopher, who remained on the floor.

"Come with me," she said. "We need to leave now. We'll walk through the woods and avoid the road. I know the way."

Christopher took her hand and stood up without hiding his hesitation. "I still don't think this is a good idea."

"I want to be free of him," Stella said. "He's taken everything from me."

"If he stays home and finds you…"

"He won't. I told you, we'll wait until he leaves." Stella looked at him with a beseeching eye. "Trust me, please."

Christopher smiled and kissed her softly on her mouth. "You know I can't resist you, lass. God help me, I can't say no to you." He raised her hand to his lips and kissed it. "I just pray this isn't a mistake."

Stella smiled as much as her swollen lip would allow. "It isn't a mistake. Nothing will go wrong," she said. "And we'll be on our way to Savannah in no time."

They slipped out of the shack and glanced around the docks to make sure they were alone. Without a word, Stella and Christopher walked quickly to the road and, together, they disappeared into the trees.

****

"What's going on?" Christopher whispered as he and Stella stared through the trees at the Winslow home.

"I can't imagine," Stella said.

The Chilmark police wagon was parked in front of the house, and two men Stella recognized as Jon Coffin and Zebediah Johnson paced on the porch Josiah had so harshly thrown her on the night before. The two men looked edgy and angry as they walked the length of the porch and back, and she could see them shaking their heads as if in disbelief.

Stella knew Johnson and Coffin regularly came to Josiah to purchase medications from him, and in fact they were among the best customers of the drug store he ran out of his office. She cursed herself for forgetting this was the morning they normally came. Josiah would likely not be leaving today for patient visits at all. But with the activity going on around her home, she knew Josiah's schedule was the least of her concerns at the moment.

"I need to find out what's going on," she whispered. "I'm going over there."

"Wait, Stella," Christopher said. "What if Josiah has set this up somehow? What if he wants to get you in trouble?"

"For what? I've done nothing that would concern the police. Something's happened in my home and I mean to find out what it is."

Stella walked through the trees towards the road with Christopher reluctantly following behind.

"What's happened here?" she called out.

Johnson and Coffin turned to her and stared open mouthed at both Stella and her companion.

"It's him," Jon said. "The mucker!"

"What?" Stella said. "What are you on about?"

Jon stuck his head inside the door of the house. "Sheriff? Casey's out here right now. He's bold enough to show his face at the doc's home."

Christopher froze at the gate of Stella's home. He couldn't imagine what had happened, but he knew at once that he had made a terrible mistake in coming to the Winslow home. He turned, hoping to run back to the safety of the woods, but he was tackled to the ground before he could move more than a yard.

Zebediah Johnson shoved Christopher from behind and quickly jumped on top of him, pinning his arms behind his back before Christopher could fight him off.

"I've got him, Sheriff!" he yelled out.

"What are you doing?" Stella yelled. "Let go of him!"

Christopher struggled under the weight of his captor. "Let me go, man. I've done nothing to ye."

"Nothing to me, no. But plenty to the doc. You dirty Irish son of a bitch."

"What are you talking about? I've not even seen Doctor Winslow in months."

Stella saw Sheriff Tilton come onto the porch and ran to him. "What on earth is happening here? Tell Mr. Johnson to let Mr. Casey go at once."

The sheriff stopped short, obviously taken aback by the wounds to Stella's face. He caught himself, and tipped his hat. "I'm afraid I can't do that, Mrs. Winslow."

"Where is my husband? What's going on?"

"The doc's dead," Jon said. "And that mucker killed him."

Stella reeled backwards as if she had once again been punched.

"Damn you, Coffin, keep your mouth closed for once," the sheriff said. He removed his hat and looked at Stella with pity. "I'm afraid it's true, ma'am. Doctor Winslow's been murdered. The boys here found him inside this morning."

"He was dead when we got here," Jon said. He pointed again at Christopher, who continued to struggle with Zebediah. "Shot in the chest by that Irish bastard."

Stella shook her head and felt so dizzy she feared she would collapse. "It can't be true," she said. "It's not true."

Sheriff Tilton turned to Jon and gestured towards the two figures on the ground. "Go help Zebediah rein that one in," he said. As Jon ran off the porch, Tilton turned his attention back to Stella.

"I'm afraid it is true, ma'am. I'm truly sorry."

Stella stared up into his eyes. "But you're not listening to me. It can't be true. Christopher didn't shoot Josiah. He couldn't have."

"Ma'am, your husband wrote out a note before he passed. He named Mr. Casey there as his killer."

Stella felt herself slipping, and grabbed onto the railing of her porch for support.

"Oh no," she cried. "No, please."

"I'd recommend you not go inside your house. I'm sending another officer out here to help and he'll take you to a safe place."

A safe place. She had been safe. She was safe with Christopher, and she'd led him here to this.

"He was with me," Stella said. "He didn't shoot Josiah."

The sheriff looked at her with pity, and walked off the porch towards Christopher, who was now trapped between Jon and Zebediah. The sheriff took a rope from his belt, and tied Christopher's hands together in front of him. He led him towards the back of the police wagon.

"No!" Stella yelled. "Please listen to me. You're making a terrible mistake. He was with me!"

Stella ran until she found herself restrained by both Jon and Zebediah.

"Let go of me," she yelled. "Let go of me!"

Unable to break free, she stood helplessly as Christopher was shackled to the police wagon.

"No, please," she cried out. "NO!"

2013

"*He* didn't do it," Hannah said. "I'm sure of it."

"What are you talking about, Hannah?" Sarah asked.

"What do you mean, what am I talking about? Haven't you been listening to me at all?"

Sarah leaned back in her office chair. She couldn't deny that she had been paying more attention to the stack of files on her desk than to Hannah's voice in her ear. She felt bad about it, but that's how it was.

"I'm sorry, I got distracted. I'm at work, remember?" Sarah let out a deep breath. "But I know it's about those people you've been reading about."

"Yes, the people I've been reading about." Hannah rolled her eyes. "The people who are going to be the subject of my book! I thought you could pay attention for five minutes at least."

"I'm paying attention now, okay? I told you I was sorry. Now what is it? Who didn't do what?"

Hannah sighed and tried to hide her irritation. "Christopher Casey didn't kill Josiah Winslow. I know now he was arrested for it, but I'm certain he didn't do it. That has to be what this is all about."

"What what is all about?"

Hannah rolled her eyes. "The reason I'm here! Stella Winslow, the ghost. I know this is what she wants me to find out. This is why she brought me here."

"Hannah, do you have any idea how crazy you sound?"

"No, Sarah, I don't. But thanks so much for pointing it out."

"I'm sorry, but you know it's the truth. You go all the way to the Vineyard because of some woman on a webcam..."

"All the way to the Vineyard? From Boston? You make it sound like I've crossed the world. It's not exactly a long trip."

"Whatever. That's beside the point and you know it. I'm worried about you with this whole situation. It's like you've become obsessed with some wild goose chase."

"You're right about one thing. I am obsessed with Stella and her story. I want to find out what happened to her. But it's not a wild goose chase. It's a story that's been waiting for centuries to be told."

Sarah paused and bit her lip, unsure how to proceed. "Hannah, whatever else is going on here, I'm worried about you."

"Why?"

"Because you haven't been yourself since you quit your job. I think spending all of this time on your own has brought up too many bad memories for you."

"You mean memories of my parents? The accident?"

"I think so, yes. I think that's why you were so drawn to the Vineyard."

Hannah let out a deep breath. "I know your concern is genuine and I appreciate that. But may I remind you that you work in marketing? You're not a psychiatrist. So spare me the analysis, please."

"Fine, Hannah, fine. I give up. Tell me all about these people from the 1800s you simply have to write about."

"I've already told you. Someone killed Stella Winslow's husband and Christopher Casey was the one arrested for it. Somebody framed him."

"So what happened to him after that?"

"I don't know yet. The damn library keeps closing on me before I can get everything I need. But I'm going back tomorrow." Hannah paused. "Whatever happened to him, I doubt it was good. An Irish immigrant wouldn't have had a lot of friends on the Vineyard back in those days. And the doctor was a respected member of the island community."

"How do you know again that this Irishman was framed?"

"I just know it. That has to be the story Stella is trying to tell me."

"Oh my God. Back to the ghost."

"Yes, Sarah, back to the ghost. Scoff at me all you want. I'm telling you the truth."

"If you say so."

Hannah scowled and decided to change the subject. "Have you seen Jon?"

"Jon? Why would I see him?"

"I don't know. Just thought when you were out and about you might run into him."

"No, I haven't. Why?"

"No reason. I haven't spoken with him. He said he thought my trip here was so stupid he didn't want to hear anything about my lunacy. I told him that was fine because I have no desire to discuss it with him anyway." Hannah paused. "I really need to just break it off with him once and for all."

"Well, truer words were never spoken there. You know that's what I've thought for a long time. He's a jackass, Hannah. I'm sorry, but he is."

"No, no need to be sorry. You're right. He is, in fact, a jackass." Hannah couldn't keep the smile out of her voice as she talked.

"At least we're clear on that," Sarah said, grinning.

Hannah laughed. "Yeah, that's something most people can agree on." She let out a breath and scanned the Oak Bluffs harbor where she was again enjoying a lobster roll from Sandy's.

"I should get back to work," Sarah said, "I need to have this report finished tonight."

"Okay, I'll let you go. I'll be home soon anyway. I need to get back to Boston to meet with a potential client. He wants me to ghostwrite for him and I think I'm going to take him up on it."

"You're really obsessed with ghosts now, aren't you?"

"What?"

"Stella the ghost. Ghostwriting…" Sarah paused. "Okay, it was a lame joke."

Hannah chuckled. "You're right, it was."

"Alright, well, I hope you find what you're looking for there."

"Thanks. I do too."

Hannah closed her phone and slipped it back into her pocket. She tried to ignore Sarah's feeling that she was nuts for pursuing this story, but it bothered her all the same. To her, what was going on seemed so obvious. Why couldn't her friend see that?

Or was Sarah right that she wanted to be involved with something on the Vineyard so she could feel connected to her parents? Hannah shook her head. No, that wasn't it. If she simply wanted to feel connected to her parents, she could travel home to Indianapolis. This was about more than that.

Hannah finished her dinner and paid her check before getting back in her car to once again return to Chilmark and the Hammett House. She felt tired and agitated when she arrived and couldn't wait to stretch out on her bed and retire for the night. But her room had other plans.

As Hannah walked in the door of her room, she immediately felt a chill. Assuming she had simply left the window open and the evening air had cooled the room, she crossed the room to the window, only to find it already closed.

She froze where she stood, suddenly feeling as if there was something else going on in the room. There was a presence there. And it was something way beyond a chill.

Almost certain of what she would find, Hannah slowly turned towards her bed. Sure enough, a sheet of paper had been left up against her pillows. Hannah could feel her heart pounding in her chest as she walked to the bed and picked up the paper with a trembling hand.

It was a Boston Globe article from 1884 about a prominent doctor in the city who had committed suicide by shooting himself in the head. The act had been a total shock to the patients and friends of the man as all had considered him to be an excellent doctor and a stable, happy person. The doctor had left a note apologizing to his wife for his actions. He had apparently been driven to suicide by his gambling debts and addiction to laudanum.

Hannah dropped onto the bed and stared at the paper. She realized she had been holding her breath since entering the room and breathed deeply as she studied the words on the page.

Hannah knew beyond all doubt that Stella was behind this. But why? What did the suicide of a doctor in Boston have to do with her story? Had someone in Stella's life committed suicide? If so, who? Hannah looked up and glanced around the room, suddenly conscious that someone or something else may still be there. But she was alone, and nothing else had been left for her to find.

She stared back at the paper and tried to make sense of the latest clue she had been given. Had Christopher committed suicide after he was arrested? Or perhaps Stella has taken her own life? Hannah shook her head. No, that didn't make sense. Why would she be so intent on having the story of her own suicide told?

Hannah kicked off her shoes and changed from her clothes into her pajamas. She pulled back the covers of her bed and ducked under them leaving the strange article on her bedside table. All feelings of fatigue and tiredness were gone, and she stared at the ceiling in her now dark room and tried to understand what Stella was trying to tell her.

"Can't you ever just come and talk to me?" she said into the dark, only half kidding. "I'm right here. You can just come in and tell me what you want me to know."

Hannah scoffed at herself and knew full well that if a ghost of any sort suddenly appeared and started talking to her she would likely have a heart attack. And then she would commit herself to the psychiatric ward.

No, that wasn't the answer. She knew Stella was giving her all the help she was able to give. Now it was up to her to return to her research and find out the whole story.

She felt a sense of unease as she contemplated returning to the periodical index and finding the newspaper articles on the arrest and trial of Christopher Casey. She wasn't sure if she wanted to know what Stella was trying to tell her now.

She was afraid to find out which player in this long-ago drama had taken his or her own life.

****

1884

The makeshift courtroom in the Tisbury Town Hall bustled with anticipation as the hastily assembled grand jury met to decide whether or not to indict Christopher for the murder of Josiah Winslow. In spite of the fact that Josiah had died in Chilmark, the court proceedings had to be held in Tisbury as Chilmark did not have its own courthouse. Tisbury didn't either, but was still one up on Chilmark as Chilmark didn't even have a town hall where the jury could convene.

Spectators filled the town hall and crowded along the walls, jamming the hall to such an extent that some were left to line up outside and strain to hear the goings-on inside the building. Stella had arrived early, well before any crowd had started to assemble, so she could be assured of a front row seat. In fact she had found the courtroom empty when she had arrived which was to her liking. She knew very well how much the typical islander loved any sort of court affair, and any proceeding was liable to be turned into a complete spectacle due to many islanders viewing it as entertainment. She couldn't deal with being in the thick of the crowd today. And, she wanted to be able to stare straight ahead and see nothing but the court participants. That way, she would not have to see her neighbors staring at her.

The crowd noise dulled to a whisper as the judge entered the court and Christopher was led in, accompanied by a deputy on either side of him. Stella felt as if she had been punched in the stomach when she saw him. He was pale and gaunt, and his eyes were as wide as saucers. He was clearly frightened and, while she desperately wanted to think otherwise, Stella knew perfectly well that he had good reason to be. He had no chance in this folly of a judicial proceeding.

Stella resisted the urge to roll her eyes at the "judge," who until last week had been no more than a grocer in Vineyard Haven. As this was the first murder case to be considered in Tisbury, his appointment to the bench had been out of necessity. In years past, all island judicial matters had been settled in Edgartown, but the "up islanders" had decided they needed a judicial seat of their own. Stella felt sure that this was merely to make sure that the grand jury was filled with as many of Josiah's friends as possible.

The judge called the proceedings to order and demanded silence from the crowd. Stella scowled as the prosecuting attorney explained his case against Christopher, citing the testimony of John Coffin and Zebediah Johnson, the note written in Josiah's hand that named Christopher as the killer, and the statements of Mrs. Poole and others in Menemsha who had seen Stella and Christopher together. The crowd roared when Christopher's attorney introduced Christopher's alibi, and Stella's sworn testimony that he had been with her when Josiah had died and therefore could not be the killer. Stella felt her cheeks burning at the sounds of laughter and guffaws echoing around the hall. Her status as a "hussy" and the islanders' determination that she was now a loose woman made her testimony useless to Christopher.

The spectacle was over before it began, and the jury came down with an indictment of murder in the first degree. Christopher was to remain in the custody of the Tisbury sheriff until such time as he could be transferred to New

Bedford where he would stand trial. Stella forced herself to block the crowd's cheers from her mind and to focus only on Christopher. He looked lost and stunned as the deputy shackled his hands behind his back and led him out of the hall. Stella tried to catch his attention and let him know she would fight for him, but his eyes remained downcast until he disappeared from the room.

Stella remained in her seat until the last spectator had left and she was once again alone in the courtroom. She held her purse in her lap and stared at the now abandoned tables in front of her. She was still unable to see clearly out of her right eye, thanks to Josiah's punch, and her abdomen still throbbed from his kick. She knew she shouldn't be surprised, but she still found herself incredulous that in the aftermath of Josiah's death not one of her fellow Vineyarders had shown an inkling of concern for her own injuries. She had even heard talk that she had deserved whatever beating she had received due to her affair with Christopher. No one was interested in her side of the story.

But it wasn't herself that she was worried about now. No matter how much her neighbors now hated her, she wasn't in any danger. Christopher was the one to be concerned about. In fact, concerned wasn't nearly a strong enough word. Stella was terrified for him.

Worse, she blamed herself for what had happened and, even if Christopher didn't hold her responsible, she would always know the truth. It had been her idea to return to her home. If she had listened to Christopher, the two of them would be on the mainland now, and Christopher would have found a job on the docks. She could have found a job cleaning and they would already be saving money to go to Savannah.

If she hadn't insisted on going home to get her money, none of this would have happened. No matter what happened to Christopher from this point forward, and she couldn't imagine it would be anything good, she would never forgive herself for that simple fact.

Stella finally stood up from her seat, her legs cramped after hours of sitting in one position. She had a long walk home, and no longer felt safe walking alone in the dark. With the cat-calls and hoots that had been sent her way, she wouldn't put anything past the men who had once been her friends.

She cared little for her own welfare, but she still couldn't risk anything happening to her that would hamper her ability to help Christopher. He had no one but her on his side, and she had no intention of abandoning him. Tomorrow, she would take Grover and visit him in the jail cell that had been built in the bottom of the town hall. She'd bring him some baked goods just as she had in Menemsha. She'd make sure he knew he wasn't alone.

And, above all else, she'd figure out a plan to get him free.

****

Stella was exhausted by the time she returned to the home she had lived in her entire life and now despised. The house reeked of Josiah, and she couldn't even look at her kitchen without feeling the blows he had so brutally rained on her face.

As she had done nearly every night since Josiah's death, she retreated to his office and, ignoring the blood stains that remained on the floor, sat at his desk. She turned everything she had seen and been told about what happened over in her mind while desperately trying to figure out who had really killed her husband and framed Christopher.

Josiah's safe and medicine chest had been untouched, and the police had ruled out robbery as a motive. And there had been no signs of forced entry into the Winslow home. The sheriff had made it clear that he had no reason to doubt that the note was authentic and that Christopher was in fact the killer.

Stella knew that there was only one person besides herself and Christopher who knew that wasn't true, and that was the person who had actually killed Josiah. And exactly what would make that person come forward and implicate themselves in such a crime?

Shaking her head, Stella knew the only hope of discovering the truth lay with her. But she had no idea how or where to start. As much as she now despised Josiah, she couldn't deny that the man had been a good doctor who was well-liked among his neighbors and his patients. What reason would anyone have to kill him?

Stella got up from the desk and sank to the floor. Tears formed in the corner of her eyes, and fell like rain drops onto the wooden floorboards around her. She let out a deep breath and tried to find the energy to get up and retire to bed. There was nothing else she could do today.

She glanced at the stack of newspapers Josiah had always kept next to his desk. She was grateful that the stack of papers was old now, as there was no way she would want to read the current editions. She could only imagine the vitriol and hatred published about Christopher. She reached for one of the papers, desperate to return to a time before this nightmare started, if only in her mind, and inadvertently knocked several to the floor.

Stella felt her eyes once again well with tears as she saw the Boston Globe Christopher had brought her from Cottage City among the scattered papers. She picked it up in her hands and held it to her chest, remembering the night in the barn when Christopher had given it to her. She had read each word of the paper in the following days, starting with the story of the doctor who had committed suicide in Boston.

Stella stood up and, still cradling the paper, started to leave the room. As she got to the doorway, she stopped short, and the paper fell to the floor. Feeling lightheaded, Stella grabbed one of the chairs Josiah had kept for patients and sunk slowly into it.

She stared down at the paper and the story of the Boston doctor staring back at her. Could it be possible?

Stella heard Josiah's harsh voice in her head as he'd tossed her outside on her porch and kicked her as if she was no better than a stray dog.

"I'm not finished yet, Stella. You'll see."

It could definitely be possible and, more than that, Stella knew it was true. Stella knew now what had happened to Josiah. She knew who had killed her husband, and why. The answer was staring her in the face. It had been right here in her home all along.

****

Stella saddled Grover and climbed onto his back to make the journey to the Tisbury Town Hall and the jail cell in its basement. She could have made the trip on foot, but she always made sure to ride Grover when she visited Christopher. That way it wouldn't be suspicious if anyone should happen to see her when she arrived for her final visit on horseback.

She had packed baked goods in the saddle bags that hung on Grover's side, enough for both Christopher and whomever was guarding the cell during her visit. She also made sure to pack plenty of carrots for Grover. It calmed her nerves to be able to nuzzle the horse and feed him his favorite treat.

After arriving at the hall, Stella hitched Grover up to the post outside the building and gave him a carrot to tide him over until she returned. She walked inside and made her way to the basement, where she saw Zebediah Johnson sitting beside the door to the jail room. She knew she would find either Johnson or Jon Coffin standing guard over Christopher. They had made it their mission to be involved in the case since they had discovered Josiah's body and played a role in capturing Christopher. It made no difference to Stella which one was on duty when she visited. She loathed them both equally.

"Good day to you, Mrs. Winslow," Zebediah said, the customary sneer in his voice.

"And to you, Mr. Johnson."

"What did you bring for us today?"

Stella removed a small loaf of sweet bread from her bag. "For you," she said.

"That all? I don't doubt you've got more in that bag for your boyfriend."

"I've brought bread and cheese for Mr. Casey, if that's who you're referring to."

Zebediah chuckled. "Oh, come on now Stella. What's the point of playing games now? Everyone on the island knows what you've been up to with this mucker."

Stella bristled at his use of her Christian name without her consent. The lack of respect her life-long neighbors now showed her became more glaring each day. She reminded herself that she didn't really care. Her hatred of them far outshone any contempt they had for her.

"I'd like to visit with the prisoner now if there's no objection, Mr. Johnson," she said, keeping her voice steady.

"No objection on my end." Johnson got up from his chair and yelled across the room at Christopher. "What about you, Mick? You object?"

Stella ignored him and walked to the cell and Christopher. She kept her gaze on him and forced her face into a smile.

"How are you today?" she asked.

"Much better now that you're here."

Stella pulled a nearby chair up to the cell and removed the food and a canteen of well water from her bag. "I've brought you lunch," she said.

Christopher sat down on the floor of his cell and reached through the bars for the food and drink. "Thank you," he said.

Stella chatted aimlessly about her trip into town and Grover's carrot obsession until she was sure Zebediah had eaten his sweet bread and was no longer listening to her. She could see out of the corner of her eye that he was now leaning back against the wall with feet propped up on the stairs leading to the main floor. He had pulled his hat over his eyes and looked to be asleep. Still, Stella didn't chance it, and kept her voice to a whisper.

"I've got everything arranged," she said. "Grover and I will be here for you tomorrow night."

Christopher's eyes widened. "Really? I never dreamed it would be so soon."

"I don't know when they're planning to transfer you to New Bedford. It could be any day now. We don't have time to waste."

"So what is your plan, Mrs. Winslow?"

Stella let out a deep breath and smiled at him. She didn't want him to see any fear on her face. It would all work out, she was sure of it.

"I've found the bromides in Josiah's medicine chest. I'll put enough in the cake I make to sedate whichever reprobate is here guarding you." She gestured with her eyes towards Zebediah. "I actually put a little in his cake today just to test it and look how he's sleeping there."

Christopher glanced at his guard. "He does seem to be out, doesn't he?"

"He is," Stella said. "And whichever one of them is here tomorrow will be too. I'll bring the cake for him late in the afternoon and he'll sleep for hours, I'll make certain of that. I'll come back for you as soon as it's dark. I can take the key to the cell from your guard while he's sleeping. Then we'll ride Grover to Gay Head. Mr. Mayhew and the Indians will have a boat waiting for us."

Christopher raised his eyebrows. "They're willing to help me?"

"You know how fond Mr. Mayhew is of you. And the Indians don't put much stock in islanders' ideas of justice."

Stella glanced over at Zebediah and turned back to Christopher. She slipped her hand through the bars and felt a sense of peace pass through her as he took her petite hand in his own. She knew her plan was going to work.

"We'll take the Indians' boat to Cottage City and slip onto one of the freight boats," she said. "No one will notice us. We can hide in the hold. And I know it's a short trip to the mainland. My father went to New Bedford once. He told me all about the trip when he returned."

Christopher caressed her hand with his roughened fingers. "Are you sure you want to do this, Stella? If they catch us…"

"They won't catch us," Stella said firmly. "And yes, I'm sure."

"I hate to put you at risk."

"You're not putting me at risk. I'm doing it to myself. And, what choice do I have, anyway? Do you expect me to just ignore the fact that I'm the reason you're locked up here like an animal?"

"Don't say that," Christopher said, shaking his head. "You're not to blame."

"Of course I am. If not for me, you never would have been anywhere near my house when they found Josiah. You know it's true, so don't condescend to me by pretending it isn't."

Christopher couldn't help but smile. "Yes ma'am." He paused and let out a breath. "But they would have found me soon enough whether I'd been there at the house with you or not. Don't blame yourself."

"I shall blame myself. You wanted to run, Christopher. By the time those idiots found Josiah's body we could have already been on a steamer to New Bedford."

"Alright, lass. I know better than to argue with you."

"Good."

"And I know when it's time to change a subject." Christopher waved his hand around the small cell. "But I'm afraid there's not much to talk about here in my new home."

"We don't have to talk," Stella said as she caressed Christopher's cheek through the bars she longed to snap in two. "We can just sit together."

"We can, but I like the sound of your voice, love. I miss it when you're not here." He kissed Stella's hand and turned his face towards hers. "So tell me. Since you know these islanders a damn sight better than I do, who do you think really killed Josiah?"

Stella remained silent, pondering whether or not to share her theory.

"What is it?" Christopher asked.

Stella let out a deep breath and dropped her voice to the softest of whispers. "I think he killed himself."

Christopher couldn't hide his surprise. "What? Why would he do that?"

"Because he was ill. There was something dreadfully wrong with him and he was in terrible pain, but he'd never admit that to me. Still, there was no doubt of it."

Christopher thought back to his trip to Cottage City to pick up Josiah's medication orders. "Mrs. Luce told me he was ordering more pain medications than normal," he said. "More laudanum, I suppose."

Stella nodded. "Indeed he was. I've found a large supply stashed in one of his desk drawers. I plan to add some to my bromide cake."

"Still though. Even if the man was ill, do you really think he would shoot himself in the chest?"

"Why not, if he was dying anyway? Maybe the pain had become unbearable and he couldn't live with it anymore." Stella paused and bit her lip.

"What is it?" Christopher asked.

"When Josiah beat me, he told me he wasn't done. It was a warning, I know it. He was saying that he wasn't done hurting me. I think he wrote the note that framed you to hurt me. He didn't want me to be happy with you."

"He thought you wanted to be with me?"

"He did." Stella raised her green eyes to Christopher's. "And he was right about that."

"And he was right that I wanted to be with you too." Christopher raised Stella's hand to his face and brushed his lips against it. "My cailín álainn."

"You never did tell me what that means."

"Beautiful girl," Christopher said.

Stella blushed and brought his own hand to her lips to kiss it.

Christopher glanced around at the bars of his cell and the basement jail. "But look at us now. If you're right about Josiah's plan, I'd say he won, wouldn't you?"

"No I would not," Stella said. "I've told you my own plan and I shan't let it fail. I've got all the money from Josiah's safe and we'll be on our way to Savannah before you know it."

Christopher smiled and leaned back against the wall of the cell, holding Stella's hand in his lap. "That would be lovely."

"Not would be. It will be."

Christopher kissed her fingers one by one. "It will be. You're right."

"No one will know us there. We'll be free of all of this."

"You've convinced me. But I do have one question for you," Christopher said.

"What is it?"

"What shall become of Grover? I'm quite fond of him, I have to say."

Stella smiled. "Mr. and Mrs. Mayhew are going to take care of him. I couldn't just abandon him."

Christopher nodded. "I'm glad to hear that. He's a fine horse."

"He's the only thing left on this island that means anything to me."

"Probably time for you to leave us, Mrs. Winslow," Zebediah yelled from his chair.

Stella jumped at the harsh sound of his voice, startled that the man was apparently not sleeping as she had assumed. She had nearly forgotten he was in the room. But still, he couldn't possibly have heard her talking; she'd made sure of that. She quickly pulled her hand from Christopher's and stood up from her chair.

"Of course. I'll be on my way, Mr. Johnson."

Stella cleared her throat and stole a last glance at Christopher. "Tomorrow," she mouthed.

Christopher nodded and blew her a kiss. "Tomorrow," he mouthed in return.

Stella walked out of the basement and ascended the stairs without looking at Zebediah Johnson. She failed to notice the smirk on his face as he watched her leave the room.

****

Stella paced around her kitchen as she waited for evening to arrive. She'd delivered her precious cake filled with sedatives to Jon Coffin at the jail a few hours earlier and she had no doubt he was now sleeping soundly at his post. She only needed darkness to get Christopher out of the jail without attracting attention.

She imagined the two of them riding Grover through the woods to Gay Head on a path she'd known since she was a child and used to walk to the cliffs with her mother. She felt a rush of adrenalin and took a deep breath to calm her nerves and slow her rapidly beating heart. She couldn't let herself panic. She'd run through every detail of her plan more times than she could count, and now all she had to do was set it in motion.

Trying to steady her nerves, Stella thought of the life she and Christopher would have in Savannah. She imagined a new house near the sea and a plot of land where she could raise sheep while he worked at the nearby docks. Perhaps she would even be able to have the children she longed for and had so far been unable to carry. She was still young and had plenty of childbearing years ahead of her and she felt certain her problems would end now that she was no longer trapped with Josiah. She and Christopher could have three or maybe even four children, and a dog to snuggle at the children's feet while she read to them each night. She would be surrounded by family and would never feel alone again. Everything would be better once she was away from this island that had become such a source of pain for her.

The sun finally disappeared into the sky, and Stella left the home she had lived in for her entire life. She felt no regret as she closed the door behind her for the last time. The love she'd once felt in the home had long since disappeared. She climbed on top of Grover with her one bag of belongings swung over her shoulder and rode off towards the Tisbury town hall.

Stella knew something was wrong as soon as she and Grover reached the hall. The door to the hall was hanging open and Jon Coffin sat outside on the porch, nowhere near his post in the basement. Worse, he was wide awake and clearly not under the influence of any sedative. Stella saw her cake broken into pieces on the ground next to him. Next to the cake an unlit torch sparked on the grass, its embers still burning even though its flame had been extinguished.

"Back so soon, Mrs. Winslow?" Jon said, tipping his hat in mockery.

Stella dismounted and tied Grover to the post. "What's happened?" she asked. "Why aren't you at your post?"

"No need for me to be. No one for me to guard down there."

Stella's stomach turned over and she could taste bile rising in her throat. She walked towards the hall and broke into a run as she reached the top of the stairs and saw the basement door hanging wide open.

"Christopher?" she called out.

She heard Jon laughing behind her as she ran down the steps. "You're not going to find him down there, you stupid girl. I told you, no one's there."

Stella's blood pounded in her ears as she entered the basement and saw the empty cell in the corner.

"Where is he?" she yelled, frozen in place. "Christopher?!"

She heard footsteps behind her and swung around to come face to face with a grinning and obviously intoxicated Jon Coffin.

"How many times must I tell you, Mrs. Winslow? He's not here."

"What have you done with him?"

"Zebediah and a few others didn't think we could trust New Bedford when it came to justice on our island. You know how folks feel about the mainland."

"Tell me what you've done with him."

"Zebediah thought we should take justice for the doc into our own hands. He and the boys have merely taken your mucker lover back where he came from."

Stella shook her head, unable to make sense of the words. How could they have taken him back to Ireland? "What do you mean, where he came from?"

Before Jon could speak, Stella knew the answer to her question. It was perfectly, and horrifyingly, clear. She turned on her heels and ran back up the stairs to the outdoors, where she was grateful to find Grover still there waiting for her.

She heard Jon yelling behind her as she lifted herself into Grover's saddle.

"You and the mucker should have been quieter about your plans, Stella," he called, taunting her.

Stella cursed herself for her carelessness the previous day. She should have realized Zebediah had heard her talking. But she'd been so sure he'd been dozing from the bromide and not paying her the slightest attention.

She shook her head and forced herself to forget about the mistakes she had made yesterday. The only thing that mattered now was that she find Christopher. And she knew exactly where he was. He'd come here from *The City of Columbus*, washed up on the island thanks to the ravages of the sea. Stella knew without a doubt that Zebediah and his henchman had taken Christopher back to Gay Head.

Stella rode through the night along the path she had planned to take with Christopher, Grover's hooves thundering beneath her as she urged him to run at his fastest speed. She rounded the bend in the woods and saw the red glow of the lighthouse come into view. Her heart nearly stopped as she saw the light of torches competing with the lighthouse in the night sky. Judging by the amount of torches bobbing in the distance, Zebediah had enlisted a mob to help him go after Christopher.

"Hurry Grover, please," she cried out, digging her heels into the horse's sides. Grover neighed in response and crashed through the bushes at the edge of the path. The horse and his rider continued on into the clearing around the lighthouse.

Stella heard screams and catcalls followed by delirious laughter. She slowed Grover to a walk and tried to push down the fear exploding in her chest. She could see Christopher in the center of a group of men, his hands tied behind him and his head covered by a hood. The men pushed him forward as they waved shotguns in the air. Zebediah walked ahead of them holding a gun over his head and crying out for justice.

Stella slipped off of Grover and ran towards the crowd just as Mr. and Mrs. Mayhew emerged from the keeper's house.

"What in God's name is going on out here?" Mr. Mayhew called.

The mob stopped as one, and Zebediah turned to address Mr. Mayhew.

"Sorry to trouble you and your wife, sir. We're only here to see justice done for one of our own."

"What are ya talking about, man?"

Zebediah pointed towards Christopher with his gun. "This here mucker killed Doc Winslow. We're only making sure he pays for that is all."

Mr. Mayhew started to walk towards the group, but he was stopped short by the shotguns instantly pointed at his chest.

"We don't want no trouble with you, sir," Zebediah said. "Just leave us to our business."

Stella ran up next to Mr. Mayhew and lunged for Christopher. "Leave him alone," she screamed. "He's innocent!"

Zebediah let out a guffaw of laughter and pushed her down on the ground with a shove. "Well gentlemen, look who we have here. The mucker's hussy come to plead for his life."

Stella leapt to her feet and tried again to reach Christopher. "I will plead," she said. "You don't know what you're doing here. He's innocent! Leave him be!"

Zebediah grabbed Stella by the arm and thrust her towards two of his gang. "You fellows hold onto her. Don't let her get in my way."

He motioned for two others to keep their guns on Mr. and Mrs. Mayhew. "And you two guard the keeper and his wife here. Don't want them causing any trouble either."

"God in heaven, man," Mr. Mayhew said. "What's the matter with ya?"

Zebediah took a swig of rum and tossed the now empty bottle onto the ground next to him. "Nothing the matter with me, sir. Nothing that a dead Irishman won't cure."

Stella screamed and wrestled against the men who held her arms in an iron grip. "Please don't. Please, no!"

Zebediah laughed and removed the hood from Christopher's face. "You want a last look at him, love?"

Christopher looked at Stella with eyes wide with terror. He was unable to speak as Zebediah quickly thrust the hood into his mouth as a gag.

"I'm sorry, Christopher," Stella cried. "I'm so sorry."

Zebediah pushed Christopher towards the edge of the cliffs, pulling him up with impatience when he stumbled to the ground.

"We're just finishing what started when that ship wrecked, mucker. You should have died in the sea that night and left our doc alone."

"He didn't kill Josiah," Stella screamed, her voice crazed. "Please listen to me!"

Zebediah motioned for his man to hold Christopher tightly as he walked to his side and placed his gun against Christopher's skull.

"God help us all," Mrs. Mayhew mumbled under her breath. "Dear Lord in heaven."

"Please," Stella screamed. "Please don't!"

"This is for the doc," Zebediah said. He grinned and pulled the trigger of his gun.

Stella's screams permeated the night sky, drowning out even the sound of the crashing waves below. "No," she cried. "No!"

"Put him back where he came from, boys," Zebediah said, his face and clothing splattered with blood.

The men walked to the edge of the cliffs and tossed Christopher's now lifeless body over the side and into the pounding surf below.

Zebediah walked back towards the rest of the group with a grin on his face. He motioned towards Stella. "I dare say there's no more need to hold onto her now." He tipped his hat in a grotesque gesture to Mr. and Mrs. Mayhew. "And please take your weapons off these good folks."

The men let go of Stella and walked off with Zebediah, leaving no one remaining on the cliffs but Stella and the Mayhews.

Stella cried out for Christopher and ran towards the edge of the cliffs.

"Stop, child!" Mrs. Mayhew called. "There's nothing we can do for him now."

"Stella!" Mr. Mayhew yelled.

Stella could no longer hear the voices around her or the frantic neighing of her frightened horse. Feeling dizzy, she looked down and saw the ground swirling up to meet her. She lost consciousness and collapsed into the outstretched arms of Mrs. Mayhew.

****

2013

Hannah stared at the screen of the microfilm reader and tried to comprehend what she had just read in the newspaper reels that covered the table in front of her. The ticking of the clock on the wall above her head echoed in her ears as the rest of the library sounds faded into a vacuum around her. She couldn't say what she had expected to find when she began her quest to learn about Stella Winslow and her connection to the wreck of *The City of Columbus*. But she knew it hadn't been anything this brutal.

Hannah knew that acts of vigilantism were not a particularly rare occurrence in the early days of the Vineyard. She remembered reading a history of the island which mentioned a man who had been accused of betraying his niece and found himself tarred and feathered and tied up in a boat that was cast adrift off the coast of Gay Head. Unsurprisingly, the poor man was never heard from again. The island had been a harsh, isolated, and remote environment for centuries, and islanders believed in handling matters in their own way. While the vigilante violence was long gone, the character traits of independence and self-reliance had never gone away.

But the Martha's Vineyard Hannah had been reading about since the early morning hours was not one she could reconcile at all with the summer resort she loved so much. Still, she knew that the murder of Christopher Casey had indeed happened atop the cliffs of Aquinnah, no doubt not far from the overlook where she had spent so many summer evenings watching the sun slowly descend into the ocean below. She didn't know if she'd ever be able to look at the cliffs again without imagining the fate of Christopher Casey.

Hannah had discovered numerous accounts of the murder written by the same Boston Globe reporter who had published the story about *The City of Columbus* rescue. Chesham had covered the murder of Josiah Winslow and the resulting trial of Casey and remained on the island after Stella Winslow and the lighthouse keeper and his wife had all accused a group of vigilantes of murder. It was difficult even now to read how the accusations had been virtually ignored, and the magistrates had refused to press charges against Zebediah Johnson or his companions. It was obvious from the tone of Chesham's reports that as far as most islanders were concerned, justice had been served. Chesham had left the island in disgust, and Hannah couldn't help but share the reporter's feelings while reading his accounts more than a century later.

Hannah leaned back in her chair and stretched her arms above her head. Feeling stiff, she rolled her shoulders and tried to work out the kinks in her back. She had been sitting in the hard wooden desk chair for far too long and her body was letting her know it.

This was Hannah's last day on the Vineyard. She was scheduled to return to Boston in the morning. She had an early boat, and part of her couldn't wait to get back to the mainland and her daily life. But a bigger part of her felt disappointed that she still didn't know the whole story about Stella Winslow. The library was nearly ready to close, and Hannah didn't have the time to scroll through any more old newspapers. And even if she did have the time, she didn't have the energy to read more of the microfilm. Her eyes couldn't handle it.

But she felt agitated and disappointed because she still didn't know what had prompted Stella's ghost to make contact with her and lead her in the direction of Christopher's story. What had the suicide clue she had left on Hannah's bed at the Hammett House referred to? Hannah still didn't know who had committed suicide. Obviously, it hadn't been Christopher.

Hannah packed up her reels and returned them to the librarian at the desk. She smiled and said a quick goodbye before heading back outside to her car. She squinted as her eyes adjusted to the sunlight which now seemed harsh after so many hours inside.

Getting in her car, Hannah decided to go back to the place where this whole search had started, the Aquinnah cliffs. Perhaps there she could make sense of what she had learned and figure out what she was missing in the whole story. There was obviously something more to know about Stella Winslow and her involvement with the doomed Irishman. Hannah just needed to understand what that something was. And how to find it.

She drove to the cliffs and found a parking spot near the steps leading up to the overlook. Hannah ordered her customary cup of coffee and took a seat on the bench she had occupied when she had first come to the cliffs looking for the woman on the webcam. Staring out at the now peaceful ocean below, Hannah tried to imagine the horror of Christopher's murder at this same spot. She shivered and tried to block the scene from her mind. It wasn't something she wanted to associate with a place that to her had always been so serene.

Hannah thought back to the newspaper article about the Boston suicide that Stella had left for her as a clue. She felt frustrated once again that the ghost chose to be so cryptic. Could she not have simply written out who had committed suicide? Hannah flipped through the drama's players in her mind and stopped when she reached the image of Stella's husband Josiah. She remembered the large, beefy man who had stood so sternly at the rescue boat while Chesham took a photo. And suddenly, she thought she understood.

154

Aside from Christopher, Josiah was the only person in the story who had died. And, like the Boston doctor who had taken his own life, Josiah had clearly been a respected and trusted figure on the island. Perhaps most important of all, his death had been the reason Christopher, believed to be Stella's lover by most on the island, had been killed. According to the accounts of Christopher's arrest, Stella had loudly insisted that Christopher was innocent. And in fact she had sworn that he had been with her at the time of her husband's death. Clearly, no one had believed her.

Had Stella believed Josiah had committed suicide? Hannah took a sip of her chowder and rolled the idea around in her mind. Was this the reason Stella had made contact with Hannah? Did she want someone to know that her husband had in fact killed himself?

But why would he have done such a thing? What would make Josiah Winslow kill himself and frame someone else for his murder? She could understand wanting to frame Christopher if the reports about his affair with Stella were true. Anger and rage over betrayal and infidelity had driven many people to such cruel and desperate acts. But who would take their own life to get revenge on someone else? What could Josiah Winslow possibly have to gain from a plan that by necessity included his own death?

It didn't seem like much of a revenge plan to Hannah. In fact, it seemed completely insane to think that a man would shoot himself just to pin the murder on someone else. There were certainly better ways to avenge a grievance. But perhaps Josiah Winslow had been so blinded by rage he hadn't been thinking clearly. Or perhaps there was some other reason entirely why he would want to take his own life.

Hannah finished her coffee and took a last look at the cliffs before heading back down the steps to her car. She had to get back to her real life now, and to the work that actually paid her bills, but she had no intention of leaving the story of Stella Winslow behind. Something, call it instinct, a hunch, or perhaps another nudge from a spectral being intent on revealing the truth, told her that she needed to learn more about Josiah Winslow's death.

How she was going to learn more about the death of a man buried for 125 years was a mystery to her. But she knew it had to be done. And she knew she would figure out a way to do it.

****

Hannah walked into her Boston apartment, feeling as if she'd been gone for months instead of days. She knew as soon as she stepped through the door that something had changed.

"Jon?" she called out, setting her keys on the rack next to the door. "You home?"

She didn't expect an answer, since it would be unusual for Jon not to be at the hospital in the middle of the morning, and she didn't get one.

Hannah walked into the dining room and immediately saw a note on the table. For an instant, she thought it was Stella's ghost leaving more papers for her to read. She shook her head and laughed at her own silliness, recognizing the handwriting on the piece of paper as Jon's. Picking up the note, her chuckle quickly vanished.

"Hannah, I've moved out and am staying with Becky. I've left the furniture here for you. I think we both know this is for the best. Jon."

Short and to the point, without an ounce of affection or love. Or even of regret. Hannah tossed the note back on the table and sat down on her dining room chair. Which really was her chair. Hannah scowled at Jon's suggestion that he had been doing her a favor by leaving the furniture in the apartment. Quite big of him, since he had still been in medical school when Hannah bought 90% of the furniture in their place.

Hannah glanced around the apartment and couldn't deny that it was actually a relief that Jon was gone. And if he'd already moved in with his surgical nurse Becky, he'd clearly been involved with her for some time. Hannah had suspected this, and even questioned him about it, but he'd consistently denied it. Hannah took some comfort in the fact that she'd suspected he was lying. But she was angry that she hadn't let him know it.

Too late for that now, she thought. She let out a breath and got up from the table. Retrieving her bag from the living room floor, Hannah walked to her bedroom and unpacked the few items she had brought with her to the Vineyard. She rolled up her dirty clothes and tossed them into the hamper in her closet, put her toiletries and few cosmetics back in their home in the bathroom, and hung up her raincoat. With that, she was done unpacking.

She sat down on her bed and tried to process the fact that Jon really was gone. While she didn't think she could handle the emotional issues right now, and wanted to simply stuff them away, she knew she had to deal with the practicalities involved. For one thing, she needed to make sure the bills for the apartment were squared away. The last thing she needed was to come home and find her electricity turned off because Jon had left without paying the bill.

As Hannah ticked through the bills in her head, she realized that she actually didn't have a problem at all. The bills were all in her name, and had been since she and Jon had first moved here. He was still in school at the time, and it had made more sense to have everything in Hannah's name since she was already gainfully employed. Back then, it had seemed like a fair trade to pay the bills while he was finishing school. After all, he'd be making significantly more money once he was done and working as a surgeon and could take over his share and more then.

Sitting on her bed now alone in the apartment they had shared, Hannah couldn't believe her own stupidity. Jon had been using her for years and she had simply rolled over and allowed it. While he had indeed paid for his share of their expenses once he'd started working, he'd never made up for all the years Hannah had been their sole breadwinner. She had been an idiot, and there was no one to blame but herself. She should have kicked Jon out years ago.

Hannah glanced at the clock on her bedside table, only to find that Jon had apparently taken it with him. She guessed that the clock didn't count as furniture. She wondered what else he had decided to take when he had moved out, but she didn't have time to go looking around to find out. She'd already wasted enough time thinking about him. She only had a few hours before her appointment with her interview subject and she wanted to take a shower and get cleaned up before she left. She also had some digging around to do on her laptop.

Hannah had been thinking about Stella Winslow's story on the ferry ride back to the mainland and all during her drive back up Route 3 to Boston. She remembered a show she had watched some months back called "History's Mysteries," where a team of professionals, including a forensic anthropologist, had investigated old unsolved cases to attempt to bring some sort of resolution to them. She specifically remembered that the forensic specialist was on the faculty at Harvard. That was an easy detail to remember. She had found him so good looking while watching the show that she wished she had taken some of his classes while she was a student.

After finishing her shower, Hannah booted up her laptop and brought up the website for the "History's Mysteries" television show. She quickly brought up the cast profiles and found the man she wanted. Dr. Tim Corcoran, a professor of forensic anthropology, whose role on the team was to scientifically examine human skeletal remains. Hannah was well aware that the chances of getting authorization to exhume Josiah Winslow's remains were probably less than zero, but she had to start somewhere. And with both Harvard credibility and television clout behind him, Tim Corcoran felt like her best chance to get what she wanted. She just needed to convince him to help her first.

Hannah had found Corcoran likeable while watching the show, not only because of his drop-dead good looks but also because of his no-nonsense, down to earth demeanor. He had a slight Southern drawl and a twinkle in his brown eyes that made him appear charming even when he was discussing the grisliest of topics. Of course, his strong jawline, hint of stubble, and short brown hair with a few sophisticated touches of gray hadn't hurt either. Hannah imagined the show's producers had been beside themselves when they'd found a science geek who just happened to look like he could have worked as a model in his younger years.

As she stared at Corcoran's head shot on the website, she couldn't help but feel that he was just the person to help her with her search. He was undoubtedly besieged with requests after his work on the show, but there was no harm in trying to reach him and asking for an appointment. As a writer, she knew perfectly well that anyone who wanted a story couldn't be bashful about it. And she knew without a doubt that she wanted this story.

She glanced at the time at the corner of her screen and realized she was going to be late for her interview if she didn't get going. She brought up Corcoran's email address at Harvard and quickly wrote a short, concise message to him explaining her situation and asking for an opportunity to meet with him concerning the mystery she hoped to solve. She checked for typos and hit send, and hurried off to her appointment.

To her amazement, Hannah saw a response from Corcoran in her inbox when she returned home several hours later. He was intrigued by her story and wanted to meet her for lunch the following week at a cafe near Cambridge. Hannah knew the place and had been there many times with Jon as it was close to Massachusetts General. Amazed at her good fortune, Hannah replied immediately, thanking Corcoran for his interest and accepting his lunch invitation.

Hannah felt giddy as she walked to her kitchen and tried to figure out what to have for dinner. It was only when she got to the kitchen that she remembered she didn't actually have any food. She hasn't been to the grocery store since returning from the Vineyard that morning. She sighed when she opened the refrigerator and realized she didn't even have Half & Half for her morning coffee.

Knowing a trip to the store was unavoidable, Hannah grabbed her purse and headed back outside. She was completely exhausted and feeling the effects of her long day of travel and work, but she still felt a sense of elation about the chance to meet Tim Corcoran and discuss her theories about Josiah Winslow with him. She realized as she walked to the small grocery store around the corner from her apartment that she hadn't spent any time at all thinking about Jon and the fact that he had left her.

****

Hannah had always heard that people who are good looking on television or in the movies are actually better looking in real life. She hadn't really believed it. But then she saw Tim Corcoran. When she entered the Cambridge Cafe and scanned the restaurant looking for him, it was incredibly easy to pick him out. Sitting in a room full of young and largely attractive college students and medical residents, he was easily the best looking person in the room.

She walked to his table and introduced herself.

"Dr. Corcoran?" she asked. "I'm Hannah Forrester."

Corcoran pushed his chair back from the table and stood up to greet her. He was taller than Hannah expected, she guessed around 6'3", and, in spite of her own height, he towered over her when he shook her extended hand.

"Ms. Forrester. It's nice to meet you." He gestured towards the chair across from him. "Please, have a seat. I hope you don't mind I ordered some coffee already. I got here early."

"Oh, no, I don't mind at all."

"This place has the best coffee in Boston."

"I agree with that. I'm anxious to get some myself."

"I forgot you said you've been here before."

"Right, I have. With my..." Hannah stopped herself. She had no interest in talking about Jon, and he wasn't her boyfriend anymore anyway. "I've met friends here before."

As the waitress came to the table and asked if Hannah would like a drink, Hannah quickly ordered a coffee herself and scanned the menu in front of her while her companion asked for a refill. When the waitress returned with Hannah's coffee and a fresh pot for the two of them to share, Hannah tried to work up her nerve to approach the reason she was here in the cafe in the first place. She decided to forgo small talk and just get to the point.

"So, Dr. Corcoran..."

"Please, call me Tim."

"Of course. Tim," Hannah said. She cleared her throat. "First off I just want to say how much I appreciate your willingness to meet with me."

"My pleasure. The case you mentioned in your email sounded interesting to me. And the fact that it involves Martha's Vineyard appealed to me."

"Really? Why?"

"When I first came to Harvard as a student, I dated a girl who had family there. I visited the island with her a few times and fell in love with it. It's always stuck with me even though I haven't been there now in years."

Hannah smiled. "They say once you get the Vineyard's sand in your shoes you'll always return."

"I can definitely understand that."

The waitress returned and took their lunch orders. Hannah and Tim both laughed when they found themselves ordering the same sandwich, roast beef and cheese on a French bread roll.

"You have good taste," Tim said.

"You too," Hannah said. She took a sip of coffee and smiled at the taste she remembered quite well. "How do they make their coffee this good? I'd kill for their coffee beans."

"Careful making that kind of a statement around me. You know what I do for a living."

Hannah laughed. "You know, to be honest, I really didn't think you'd get back to me. I was sure you'd be too busy with the tv show."

Tim cocked his right eyebrow. "You haven't heard? The show was canceled."

"Oh, really? I'm sorry to hear that. I thought it was a great show."

"Unfortunately not many people agreed with you. In fact I think you and my parents are the only ones who thought so."

Hannah chuckled. "I'm sure that isn't true."

"Yeah, maybe not. My aunt liked it too." Tim smiled and took a sip of his own drink. "Honestly though, that's one of the reasons I was intrigued by your email. I found myself at loose ends a bit when we got the news of the cancellation."

"Really? So it was a surprise then?"

"We knew the show was on the bubble, but the producers were confident we'd get another season. The network had told them it was almost a certainty. So we had all of our cases arranged and I'd made room on my calendar to travel to the various locations we had lined up, only to have the network change their mind last week and give us the ax. Suddenly I had a cleared calendar and nothing to fill it with."

"I guess I had good timing then."

"You did."

"Well I'm sorry your show was canceled. But I can't deny I'm glad I caught you at the right time."

The waitress returned with their lunches and both dug in.

"So tell me more about your Martha's Vineyard mystery," Tim said between bites of his sandwich.

Hannah took another drink of coffee and launched into her tale, including her desire to write a book about the story of Stella Winslow, leaving out only the fact that she believed the ghost of Stella was somehow leading her on this quest. Instead, she pretended she had merely become interested in the story while reading about the wreck of *The City of Columbus*. She didn't want the man to think she was insane before he even considered helping with her case.

"So you don't think the Irishman killed the doctor, right?" Tim asked after she had finished.

"No, I don't. I think he was innocent and a victim of vigilantes."

Tim nodded. "I can see how that could have happened. I doubt the island was a very friendly place for Irish immigrants back then."

"I don't think anywhere in New England was particularly friendly for the Irish back then," Hannah said.

"Right. 'No Irish Need Apply' and all that."

"Exactly." Hannah let out a breath. "I think that's one of the main things that interests me about the case to tell you the truth."

"How so?"

"I grew up in Indianapolis and lived there all my life before I came to Harvard. Let's just say when I was growing up there weren't a lot of black people there. In fact, I think my mother and I were it in our neighborhood."

Tim nodded. "I know a little bit about being an outcast myself."

Hannah couldn't hide her skepticism. Was he serious? A gorgeous white man with a Harvard education?

"You?" she asked.

"Yes, me," Tim said. "Believe it or not, geeky boys from small towns in Kentucky aren't necessarily welcomed with open arms by the majority of the Harvard student body."

Hannah leaned back in her chair. "So that's where you're from, Kentucky? I noticed you had a bit of a drawl when I saw you on tv."

"I had quite a drawl when I first moved here," he said. "You should have heard some of the imitations."

"I can imagine," Hannah said. "Okay. So here's to outcasts," she said, raising her coffee mug.

"God love 'em," Tim said, clinking her mug with his own. He took another drink and finished the first half of his sandwich. "So if you don't think the Irishman killed the doctor, who do you think did? Do you have some suspect in mind from your research?"

"Yes, but I don't think it was murder. I think the doctor killed himself."

Tim paused, his coffee mug in mid-air. "Why would he have done that?"

"I don't know. But I'm hoping you can help me figure that out."

"Okay," Tim said, sounding skeptical.

"Is it possible to tell if someone shot themselves from skeletal remains?"

"If the bullet hit bone, we may be able to discern something from the angle of the shot. And sometimes we can find gun residue on clothing if it hasn't decayed. But I have to tell you, the odds are not very good."

"But not impossible?"

"No, not impossible." Tim grinned. "There's not much that's considered impossible in my line of work."

"So are you interested?"

"I haven't said I'm not."

Hannah finished her coffee and set the mug down on the table. "What would we need to do to exhume the body?"

"Well, first off, I'd need to get a court order. And work with a funeral home on the island that deals with the cemetery where the man was buried."

"It's Abel's Hill in Chilmark."

Tim nodded. "I think I remember driving past there. Creepy place."

"Yes, it is."

"We also need to make sure that no relatives object to the exhumation, but I can't imagine that will be an issue here."

"Dr. Winslow didn't have any children. There shouldn't be any descendants to object."

"Well that always makes it easier."

Hannah bit her lip. "I can hire you as a consultant but I have to be upfront, I don't have a lot of money to pay you."

"You don't have to pay me," Tim said.

"No, I should. I want to be professional about this."

"Well let's just say I'm doing this pro-bono to start."

"Why would you do that?"

"Like I told you, it interests me. And at the risk of sounding like an egotistical jackass, I really don't need the money. I might have only lasted one season on tv but that was enough to give me more money than I ever dreamed of having."

Hannah smiled. "Kentucky boy makes good."

"Yep. They wouldn't believe it back in the holler."

"Are you really from the holler?" Hannah asked, trying not to laugh.

"No. I'm from a town just outside Lexington. Everything was about basketball and bourbon and horses where I grew up, not backwoods hills."

"Well okay, so you don't need the money. I still don't feel right not paying you for your time."

"You can buy me a meal, how's that?"

"You mean you want me to pay for your lunch?"

"No, I was actually trying to find a clever way to ask you to go out to dinner with me. I'm thinking now it wasn't that clever."

"No, I think I was just being an idiot," Hannah said, blushing. "I get it now."

"Well I hope so since I just spelled it out for you."

Hannah laughed. "Alright, I'll take you to dinner. You pick the place."

"Sounds good. I'll make sure I pick somewhere expensive so you know I'm not cheap." Tim glanced at his watch and took a last swallow of coffee. "Believe me when I say Ms. Forrester..."

"Hannah"

Tim smiled. "Hannah. Believe me when I say I am very sorry to have to wrap this lunch up. But I have to get to class." He scanned the room for the waitress, frowning when he couldn't find her.

"Oh, that's okay. I'll wait for the waitress and take care of the check. That way I'll know for sure you're not cheap."

Tim laughed and stood up from the table. "Thank you. And I'll be in touch about our dinner."

"What about our case?"

"Oh sure, that too," Tim said, grinning. "I'll get started on the court order."

"Thank you."

Tim nodded and left the table. Hannah poured herself another cup of coffee and went over the lunch in her head. She couldn't actually believe he had agreed to take on the Winslow case. And she also couldn't believe how excited she was about the chance to work with him.

****

A week passed before Hannah heard from Tim again. She opened her email and found another reply to her original message to him.

"I was working so hard on being smooth I forgot to get your number. Call me."

He then added his cell and office number.

Hannah decided to take a more professional approach and dialed his Harvard office.

He answered on the second ring. "Tim Corcoran."

"Hello, Tim. It's Hannah Forrester."

"Hannah. Great to hear from you."

"Do you have news for me?"

"I do. First off, it turns out there's only one funeral home on the Vineyard, so finding out who deals with Abel's Hill was easy. It's the Hammond Funeral Home in Vineyard Haven."

Hannah remembered driving past the home hundreds of times when driving through the town, but couldn't have told anyone the name if her life depended on it. It wasn't something you paid attention to on summer vacation.

"Okay, that's good. Were you able to get a court order?"

"Yes, I was. And the Hammond people didn't give me any argument. Apparently the funeral director was another one of the select few who watched "History's Mysteries.""

Hannah smiled through the phone. "Your fame precedes you."

"It has its benefits."

"So what's next?"

"I was hoping I could take you up on that dinner offer."

"Well, okay. But what about my case?"

"I was thinking we could have dinner on the island. I have a few free days and I thought now would be as good a time as any to go see if we can figure out what happened to Dr. Winslow. Can you get away?"

"Yes, I definitely can!" Hannah couldn't keep the excitement out of her voice.

She heard Tim's chuckle on the other end of the line.

"I don't know if I've ever heard anyone so anxious to go dig up bones. Except for me, of course."

"I didn't expect to be able to go with you," Hannah said. "I'm not sure what I expected, but I guess I thought I'd just have to wait for a report from you."

"It's your story. I thought you'd want to go. Maybe seeing the process will help with your book."

"Thank you," Hannah said.

"Okay, so when do you want to go grave robbing with me?"

"Whenever you can get away is fine with me. The best thing about freelancing is that I'm flexible."

"Alright. Well, I have class tomorrow afternoon and then I'm done for the week. Want to leave Thursday morning?"

"Sure. I'll make a boat reservation. I think we'll be okay this early in the season."

"I'm counting on you to take me to the best restaurant on the island."

Hannah smiled. "I will. Let me think about it."

"Okay then. I can pick you up on Thursday morning."

"Great. I'll text you my address and a boat time as soon as I make our reservation."

"Perfect. Looking forward to it, Hannah."

"Me too. Thank you again."

Hannah ended the call and paced around her bedroom before sitting down and booting up her laptop. She couldn't resist looking at the webcam. Unsurprisingly, there was no sign of Stella on the steps leading up to the overlook.

Still, Hannah stared down at the driveway and green hills heading down to the sea and imagined that somehow Stella was there.

"I'm going to find out what really happened, Stella," she whispered. "I promise."

****

Hannah drove along South Road towards Abel's Hill Cemetery while Tim sat silently in the passenger seat and watched the passing scenery. The funeral home director drove behind them in a hearse. Hannah couldn't get over the strangeness of a hearse for a man who had been dead for more than 125 years. The closer she got to the centuries old cemetery, the more she wondered if she had made the right decision in accompanying Tim to the grave site.

It wasn't just the weirdness of digging up a long-buried corpse. She also felt darkness closing around her as soon as she and Tim had arrived at the funeral home and seen the hearse. As if no time had passed at all, she was back at the funeral home in Indianapolis, trying to maintain her composure as she made arrangements for the burial of her parents. She hadn't been near a funeral home since, and she realized now that she wished she could still say that.

Still, she had started this whole thing in motion and it was only right to see it through. Without her, neither Tim nor the funeral home workers would be spending their day digging up a grave and bringing the remains of Josiah Winslow back up to the surface. And, in spite of her personal issues, she felt certain that whatever they found in Josiah's grave was going to be the answer to the mystery of what Stella wanted her to know.

Hannah saw the cemetery coming up on the right and slowed down before putting on her turn signal and turning into the grave yard. She slowly drove down the hill towards the parking spaces, passing the grave of John Belushi on the left.

"Is that John Belushi's grave?" Tim asked.

Hannah nearly jumped in her seat. She had been so engrossed in her thoughts and Tim had been so quiet that she'd nearly forgotten she had a passenger.

"Yeah, it is," she said, wrinkling her nose at the empty beer bottles and ash trays that littered the site. "I think it's crap that people still put stuff on it like that, but it happens all the time."

"I remember reading it was here but I never saw it. I'm surprised people still leave stuff at the grave."

"It's dumb to me," Hannah said, parking the car and turning off the ignition. "And I think it's disrespectful. It's like they use it as an excuse to litter in a cemetery."

Tim nodded his head and got out of the car, glancing around at the hundreds of graves dotting the landscape.

"I bet this place is something at night," he said.

"If by something you mean creepy and spooky, you're right. You wouldn't believe what it's like here when the fog settles down in this valley." Hannah shuddered. "Creepy as hell."

"How old are the graves here?" Tim asked.

"I'm not sure, but I know there are several from all the way back in the 1700s. I guess those are the oldest, but I don't really know."

The funeral director Joe Hammond came to stand beside them.

"The Winslow grave is right up that hill," he said, pointing to their left. "We've already had workers digging there this morning so they're probably close to reaching the remains."

"Let's go join them then," Tim said.

Hannah followed behind the small group, trying her best not to look at any headstones. Instead she focused on the red maple trees that punctuated the lush greenery of the cemetery. She hadn't lied when she'd told Tim that Abel's Hill was creepy in the dark of night. But that didn't change the fact that on a sunny summer day the place was beautiful. As long as you didn't pay too much attention to all the headstones.

Hannah hated being in the cemetery, of that there was no doubt. But she had a strange sensation that Stella was there too, and that she approved of what Hannah was doing. She made sure to keep this feeling to herself, lest the rest of the group have her locked up for a mental evaluation.

They reached the grave site and waved a hello to the three workers who had been digging up Josiah's remains. Joe Hammond made introductions and all involved nodded as if there was nothing unusual involved in the scene. All except Hannah. She felt like she was in some sort of surreal dream that she would surely wake up from soon.

Josiah's headstone was at her feet, with the simple engraving "Doctor Josiah Winslow, 1843-1884" etched into its stone. As was the custom of the time, the engraving included Josiah's exact age at the time of his death - "aged 40 years, 9 months, and 3 days."

It dawned on Hannah that when she had been reading about Josiah she had imagined him as being quite old. It was odd to realize he hadn't been much older than she was now at the time of his death. And he had been younger than Tim.

The three grave diggers pulled themselves up onto solid ground and lay their shovels down at their feet.

"We've reached the remains of the poor bastard," the tallest worker said. Hannah had already forgotten his name. "The coffin's nothing but rotted wood but we should still be able to bring it up if we're careful."

The workers had an assortment of pulleys around the grave and a large gurney pulled up as close to the hole as possible.

Hammond nodded. "Great work, Stephen," he said. "Let's do it, then. I've got the hearse ready."

Stephen and one of his co-workers leaped back down into the grave and arranged their ropes and pulleys around the rotted casket. The other slowly began to turn the wheels to begin lifting the remains.

Hannah felt a combination of horror and nausea as the old casket started to come into view. Chunks of rotted wood fell off the box and back into the ground, leaving glimpses of bones in plain view. She folded her arms tightly against her chest and wondered how anyone ever got used to this kind of work. If Josiah did do what she suspected, she had no doubt that he was a miserable and horrible man. But she still felt shame and disgust at what she had set in motion. She imagined someone digging up her own parents' graves and nearly vomited on the ground. She turned away and faced the road in an attempt to regain her composure.

Tim came up beside her. "Are you okay?" he asked.

Hannah nodded. "I guess this is just harder to see than I expected."

"It's difficult, I know. Not something you ever really get used to seeing."

"I wonder if I was wrong to ask you to do this. None of this is any of my business." Hannah shook her head. "I had no right to disturb this man's remains."

Tim put his hand on her shoulder. "You wanted the truth about an old mystery. If you turn out to be right, you'll be responsible for clearing an innocent person's name."

"And what if I'm wrong?"

"Then they'll be no harm done," Tim said. He gestured towards the remains that were now being carefully placed on the gurney. "You can see that this guy's way past caring. And we'll treat the remains with the utmost respect, trust me."

Hannah let out a deep sigh and turned back towards the gurney. "This is just plain gruesome."

As if to make her point, a crow cawed and and loudly flapped his wings as he took off from a nearby headstone and lifted himself into the air. Hannah jumped.

"I told you this place was creepy," she said. "I think there are ghosts everywhere here."

"I wouldn't argue with you," Tim said.

It dawned on Hannah that she had never checked to see if Stella was also buried here in Abel's Hill. If she was, it wasn't next to her husband. Although with the circumstances of his death, she supposed that was hardly a surprise. Still, she realized that she had been so busy reading about Christopher and his fate that she hadn't thought about what happened to Stella after Josiah's death and Christopher's murder.

"You ready to go?" Tim asked. "They've got the remains in the hearse."

Hannah had been so lost in thought that she hadn't even noticed the funeral home workers moving the gurney back down to the parking lot.

"I'm more than ready," she said.

Tim smiled. "Listen, I've gotta warn you. If this upset you, I don't think you want to be there when I examine the bones. I can give you a full report afterwards. You don't need to see more of this."

Hannah shook her head. "No, no. I want to be there. I can handle it."

"If you say so."

"I do."

Hannah left the grave site and made her way back to her car with Tim following behind. She ignored the hearse and kept her attention focused on her thoughts of Stella. Whatever happened with the investigation into Josiah's remains, she had more work to do. She couldn't believe she had nearly forgotten the most important person in this long-ago tale and the whole reason she had become wrapped up in the mystery in the first place. That was a mistake she intended to rectify. She still needed to find out what had happened to Stella Winslow.

****

The embalming room in the funeral home basement reeked of antiseptic and formaldehyde, and it brought Hannah instantly back to her high school biology class and the dissections she had always loathed. There had never been any doubt in her mind that she had no interest in being a surgeon. She had enough trouble dealing with the dead frogs in front of her, the idea of a live human body was horrifying. And now she knew that a dead human body was even more difficult for her to stomach.

Josiah's remains, which were nothing more than bones and a few shreds of clothing that had somehow remained intact, were set out on an embalming table waiting for Tim to work his magic. Hannah stared at the table and felt the room starting to swirl around her. She grabbed hold of a nearby stainless steel sink to steady herself. While she knew they had been much more than bones, she knew her parents had been set out on tables identical to the one in front of her. She felt dizzy and struggled to swallow the lump that had formed in her throat.

Tim was clearly in his element and, to her immense relief, oblivious to her discomfort. He used some sort of fluid to gently clean Josiah's bones and check for signs of injury. As they knew from newspaper accounts of the time that Josiah had been shot in the chest, Tim focused on the bones of his sternum and rib cage.

Tim looked over at Hannah. "Are you okay?" he asked.

"I'm fine. Why?"

"I can show you something interesting if you don't mind coming closer."

Hannah forced her feet to start moving. "I don't mind." She leaned over Tim's shoulder. "What is it?"

"It looks to me like Josiah was shot near the heart. And since he was a doctor, I can see where if he wanted to kill himself he'd know the best place to shoot, or at least close enough to it." Tim cleared his throat. "There's a star shaped wound here on one of the top ribs near his sternum where the bullet obviously hit. That wound indicates the gun was fired from very close range."

"You mean like he fired it himself?"

"A definite possibility. And, the bullet looks to have struck the bone at an upward angle. That also points to suicide."

Hannah felt herself growing excited. "How so?"

Tim stepped away from the table and grabbed a scalpel from his table of instruments. He moved towards Hannah, who instinctively backed away.

"Don't worry," he said. "I'm not going to hurt you." He raised the scalpel. "For demonstration purposes only."

Hannah tried to relax as he came closer to her and touched the outside of her sweater with the scalpel.

"Let's say this is a gun and you're using it to shoot yourself. You're most likely to hold it like this, angling upwards and right up against your skin. Obviously if the gun was held like this the bullet would enter your body at an upwards angle." Tim moved back several steps. "But if I'm the one who is shooting you, I'm probably going to be at least a few steps away from you." He held the scalpel out straight in front of him. "And, I'm going to be holding the gun straight. There'd be no reason for me to hold it at an angle." He held the gun pointing slightly upwards. "Why would I hold the gun like this when you're standing in front of me?"

"Okay. So this is all good for my suicide theory, right?"

"Right. Although I have to caution you, you know this is all just my best guess, right? This doesn't prove anything, especially with bones this old."

"I know, I know. But I think it makes a good case."

Tim walked back over to the remains.

"There's something else here I want to have checked out."

"What's that?"

"Josiah was wearing leather gloves when he was buried, there are shreds of them left around his hands here." Tim pointed towards the skeletal hands. "Leather decomposes more slowly than any other kind of natural fabric so that's not a huge surprise."

"What do you think you can find out from the gloves?"

"If by some chance he was wearing these gloves when he shot himself, it's possible there could still be gunshot residue on them. Honestly that isn't that much of a stretch because people were buried much more quickly in those days so it's reasonable to think that he could have been buried in the clothing he had on when his body was found. Remember I told you GSR was a possibility with remains if there was any clothing left."

"I do remember. So how do you test for that?"

"I don't," Tim said. "That's not my area. But one of my colleagues back at Harvard does and I'm going to ask her to do it. I can talk to Mr. Hammond about getting these bits of leather shipped up to Harvard for testing."

"Great."

Tim continued to eye the bones, gently touching them with gloved hands. "There's something that's bothering me about these bones," he said.

"What?" Hannah asked, surprised that he sounded so puzzled.

"I can't say for sure since I'm not a medical doctor, but I feel like there's something wrong with them. They're weaker and more brittle than I'd expect. I feel like I could snap them like a twig if I wanted to." Tim let out a breath and stood up straight. "I'm going to ship the bones to Harvard as well and have them x-rayed. I want a medical pathologist to take a look at them."

"Is this allowed? Shipping the remains off the island, I mean."

"Sure. It's all part of the court order. And we'll treat them respectfully, obviously. Mr. Hammond can sign the remains over to my care, and then I'll be responsible for getting them back to him for reburial."

"So you're thinking Josiah had something wrong with him," Hannah said, more as a statement than a question. "That could give him a motive for suicide then."

"It could, but this is just a theory on my part. Like I told you, I'm not a medical doctor and I have no qualifications to make any kind of medical diagnosis."

Hannah couldn't help but chuckle. "Don't worry, I wasn't planning on quoting you and then suing you for fraud."

"Well, that's good to know," Tim said, chuckling himself.

Hannah found herself so wrapped up in the possibilities she had nearly forgotten the fact that she was in an embalming room in the basement of a funeral home - until the stench of formaldehyde hit her again and she felt a wave of nausea wash back over her.

"You okay?" Tim asked. "You suddenly look a little green around the gills."

"That's because I am," Hannah said. "I don't know how you ever get used to formaldehyde. God, what a disgusting smell."

Tim laughed. "I don't even notice it anymore."

"Well I don't just notice it, I actually feel like I'm going to vomit. I think it's time for me to get out of here."

"I'll be right behind you. I just need to set the transports up with Mr. Hammond."

"I'll wait outside," Hannah said.

"I guess this isn't a good time to ask about dinner?" Tim asked.

Ignoring his chuckle as she ran from the room with her hand over her mouth, Hannah quickly walked up the steps and outside the home where she gratefully gulped in fresh air. In spite of her nausea, she couldn't shake her excitement over Tim's findings. And, now that she was away from the stench of the formaldehyde and instead smelling the fresh sea air of Vineyard Haven harbor, she realized that she was hungry. And that she couldn't wait to have dinner with Tim.

****

Hannah had booked two rooms, one for herself and one for Tim, back at the Hammett House, and waited for him on the porch of the house now as he cleaned up after his day spent with Josiah Winslow's remains. Hannah had decided to take him to dinner at the Village Inn in nearby Menemsha. While Sandy's was her favorite place to eat on the island, the Village was the place she'd always wanted to try and never had. So she'd decided there was no time like the present and booked a reservation for two at the pricey and secluded restaurant.

She didn't regret her choice when she and Tim were seated at a window table overlooking Vineyard Sound and the Menemsha harbor. Hannah had seen more Menemsha sunsets than she could count, but none from a view quite like this. The sun was a perfectly round ball of orange in the sky, which had turned a deep shade of magenta above it. Stripes of pink danced above the dark blue water.

"It's spectacular," Tim said, taking a sip of water. Hannah had forgotten that Chilmark was a dry town and restaurant patrons needed to bring their own alcohol if they wanted drinks with their dinner. She felt like an idiot, but Tim didn't seem to care.

"It is," Hannah said. "Not many other words to describe it."

Tim had ordered lobster, while Hannah had chosen the pan seared bluefish. The waiter came to the table with their orders and placed the delectable meals in front of them.

"Can I get you two anything else right now?" he asked.

"No thanks," Hannah said. "We're good."

The two dug into their dinner and ate in a comfortable silence as both enjoyed the ambiance and the view.

"So," Tim finally said, taking a break from devouring his lobster. "What made you start researching this story for your book?"

"I told you," Hannah said. "I got the idea while researching *The City of Columbus.*"

"Yeah, but that's a hell of a leap. How do you go from a shipwreck to speculating that a doctor who treated one of the survivors killed himself?"

Hannah shrugged. "What can I say? One thing just led to another."

"Come on."

Hannah took a sip of water and stared across the table at him. "You'll think I'm crazy if I tell you the whole story."

"I doubt that."

"I think it's a safe bet."

"Come on, Hannah. You're talking to a man whose idea of a good day is spending hours with old bones. I'm not exactly the judgmental type."

"Fine. But if you think I'm nuts, just keep it to yourself."

"Deal."

Hannah sighed and told the story, beginning with Stella's appearance on the webcam. She considered leaving the old newspapers left on her bed out of it, but figured she might as well just spill the whole thing. Once you'd divulged that you made contact with a ghost through a webcam, there wasn't much point in being shy about the rest of the tale.

Tim listened intently, his brown eyes watching her quizzically. "So that's it?" he said when Hannah had finished.

"Yes. That's it."

"So what part was supposed to make me think you're crazy?"

Hannah was taken aback, until she noticed the grin on his face. "Oh, I don't know," she said, laughing. "I guess the bit about reading the old newspaper reels."

"Oh, okay. Yeah, that's batshit."

Hannah laughed again. "Alright, smartass. So what do you really think of my story? Do you think I'm batshit?"

"I don't," Tim said. "I think it's interesting."

"You do? So you believe in ghosts?"

Tim shrugged. "I don't know. But I don't just discount them." He took another bite of lobster and stared out the window as he chewed. "In my line of work," he finally said, "I've had some strange occurrences that I can't really explain. And that, frankly, I've always kept to myself."

"Like what?"

"Like I'll be working with a set of remains and somehow I get the feeling that the person these bones used to be is trying to help me see the truth about their deaths. If I'm alone in a room with the bones, I almost start to feel like there's someone there with me. I can sense a presence."

Hannah's eyes widened. "When I found the newspaper on my bed back at the Hammett House, I felt like there was someone with me in the room."

Tim nodded. "So you know what I mean."

"I guess so." Hannah stared across the table at him as he took more of his lobster. "I have to admit, I'm surprised you're interested in this sort of thing."

"Why?"

"Because you're a scientist. I thought science was all about things that can be explained."

"It is. And that's what I look for in the bones. Explanations to what happened in the past."

"Still. It's surprising."

Tim shrugged. "I guess I'm just a different kind of scientist. And you remember how I told you I grew up around Lexington?"

"Sure."

"Like I told you, I didn't grow up down in the holler. But that doesn't mean I didn't have relatives there. I had a great-aunt who lived out in the hills and she was one of the best storytellers I've ever known. I loved visiting her because she'd tell me all about the ghosts in the hills and the legends..." Tim smiled fondly. "Crazy shit, but I never doubted her that some of it was true. When you're in a place as steeped in history and lore as the Appalachian Mountains, you have to respect that there are things we can't really explain about the people who've been there before us."

"And might still be sticking around?" Hannah asked.

"Exactly."

Hannah leaned back in her chair and smiled at him. "I have to admit, it's really refreshing to talk to you. I've only told a few people about this story, but they've thought I was crazy as can be."

"Well, maybe we're both headed for the nuthouse together."

Hannah stared out at the Sound below them, remembering testimony she had read from Christopher's indictment that he had disappeared from his employer's home at Menemsha on the night of Josiah's death. She thought about him working on the docks and looking at the same ocean and sky she was looking at now. She wondered if he had ever walked along the jetties that lined the channel the way she had with her father when she was a kid. Not for the first time, she wished she had a picture of him in her mind like she did the others.

There was something sad about the fact that he would always be a faceless young man.

"Penny for your thoughts," Tim said.

Hannah turned away from the window and back to her dinner companion. "I was just thinking about Christopher. During my research into the case I learned that he worked on the docks in Menemsha. So he would have been looking at the same view we are at some point. Or at least close enough."

"So why do you think Stella made contact with you?" Tim asked.

"I don't know. But I think she just wants the story of what happened to come out, even after all this time."

"But why you?"

Hannah remembered the sense she had from the articles she had read, that Stella was alone except for her husband. Through time, she somehow sensed a kindred spirit in Stella. Maybe Stella felt the same way about her.

"I think maybe she just thought I might be someone who could understand her." Hannah let out a deep breath. "My parents were killed a few years ago in a car accident and I don't have any siblings so I've been pretty much alone ever since."

"I'm sorry."

"Thanks. I think Stella felt alone in her life except for her friendship with Christopher Casey. I think maybe she thought I'd feel a connection to her."

"Do you?"

Hannah shrugged. "Maybe. I don't really know. I know I felt something when I saw her on that webcam though. She just looked so sad and lost..." She paused and suddenly looked across the table at Tim.

"What?" he asked.

"When we were at the cemetery earlier it dawned on me that even if I learn what happened to Josiah, I still don't have the whole story."

"How so?"

"I have no idea what happened to Stella. I hadn't thought about it because I was so wrapped up in the murder of Christopher, but I wonder what happened to her. What kind of a life could she have had after such a tragedy? Plus, she was accused of infidelity and it was clear that the majority of her neighbors believed she had been unfaithful to her husband."

"That would have been a hell of a scandal back then," Tim said.

"How could she have kept living here after all that?"

"Maybe she didn't."

Hannah nodded, suddenly feeling a rush of adrenalin. "I need to find out," she said. She wiped her face with her napkin and set it on the table next to her plate as she glanced around the restaurant for the waiter.

"Can we finish dinner first?" Tim asked. "I don't think you're going to be able to find much out tonight."

Hannah laughed. "I'm sorry, you're right. I just got excited for a minute."

"I noticed."

"Would you like to get dessert?"

"I'd love it," Tim said. "But I don't feel right about you paying for my meal here. We'll split the bill."

"We absolutely will not. I made a deal and I'm sticking with it."

"Okay, you win. But let's do this again back in Boston."

"Do what?"

"What do you mean, do what? Dig up an old grave, of course."

Tim laughed at the look on Hannah's face. "I'm kidding. I meant let's go out to dinner again, that's all."

Hannah turned red, embarrassed at her momentary cluelessness. "I'm sorry, I should have known what you meant. I can be a little slow sometimes." She smiled across the table. "I'd love to have dinner with you again."

"Good. And next time will be my treat."

"Kind of defeats the purpose of our deal."

"Who cares? I told you all along I didn't need money to work on your case. This kind of thing is what I consider entertainment."

"No wonder you don't think I'm batshit."

"Exactly. Didn't I tell you I have no room to judge?"

The waiter returned with their desserts and Hannah leaned back in her chair, studying Tim as he took a bite of his chocolate bread pudding. She had made sure to check out his left hand when she'd first enjoyed lunch with him, and had been happy to see then that he didn't wear a wedding ring. But she knew perfectly well that that didn't necessarily mean he wasn't married. She couldn't deny she hoped he wasn't and decided to find out.

"So tell me more about yourself," she said. "What do you do when you're not digging up bones?"

"Well you already know I teach. Besides that, I love baseball."

"Red Sox?"

"Cincinnati Reds."

Hannah nodded, pleased. "I should have guessed that since you're from Kentucky. I'm a Colts fan to the core and have never switched to the Patriots, so I can relate." She took a bite of her lemon cake. "What else do you love?"

"Dogs. I have two of them. A mutt named Harris and a golden retriever named Lucy."

"I had a dog as a kid," Hannah said. "I've always wanted one here but my apartment doesn't allow them and for years I've been too lazy to move." Hannah finally decided to stop beating around the bush. "Do you have children in addition to your dogs?"

Tim shook his head. "No, no children. You probably want to know if I'm married, right?"

"The question crossed my mind."

"I'm divorced, to answer your question. Have been for three years now."

"I'm sorry."

"Don't be. It was the best thing for both of us." Tim shook his head. "If I was married and I was sitting here having dinner with you and asking you to dinner back in Boston, I hate to think what an asshole I'd have to be to be doing that."

Hannah laughed. "I'm sorry, I didn't mean to imply you're an asshole. But you can never be too careful. And for the record, I'm not married either."

Tim chuckled and shook his head. "Alright. Glad we got that out on the table."

The sun had disappeared into the sea now, and Hannah stared out the window at the darkness descending on the harbor. She suddenly felt awkward and ready to be done with dinner. She hadn't meant for this to turn personal. It was only supposed to be about her book.

"I should probably get the check," she said. "I'm just realizing what a long day it's been."

"It has been that. But this dinner was a great way to end it."

Hannah blushed at the grin Tim shot her across the table. She forced herself to ignore the fact that he was so good looking he nearly made her short of breath. She had no desire to act like a silly schoolgirl and throw herself at him. She had no doubt he was used to women doing exactly that when they saw him. She didn't have the energy for that now after all that had happened with Jon.

And this was only supposed to be about her book.

****

Hannah busily typed away on her keyboard, anxious to make an afternoon deadline. She scowled when her phone vibrated on her desk, but the scowl turned to a smile when she picked the phone up and saw that her caller was Tim.

"Hi Tim," she said.

"Good morning. Did I catch you at a good time to talk?"

"Sure," Hannah lied. "What's up?"

"I have some test results from my colleagues that I think will interest you."

"Already?"

"Of course. None of these tests take very long."

Hannah could hear her heart beating in her chest and her palms felt clammy. She had put the Winslow case out of her mind since returning from the Vineyard with Tim and had focused on her work, but now that the answers to her questions might be at hand she was suddenly a nervous wreck.

"Okay," she said, taking a deep breath. "What do you have for me?"

"Well for one, there were minute traces of gunshot residue on the remains of the leather gloves."

"Really? So that shows he fired the gun?"

"It shows he fired a gun while wearing those gloves. We can't definitively determine that it was the gun that killed him."

"Well, come on, Tim. What other gun would it be?"

"We can't say for sure. I'm just making that clear."

"Alright. Any other results?"

"Yes. I haven't even told you the most interesting one yet. My friend ran tests on the bones. Josiah Winslow was riddled with bone cancer when he died."

Hannah remained silent, stunned at the news.

"Once again, we can't say anything for sure," Tim continued, "but the cancer was so extensive that my friend's guess is that it metastasized from somewhere else in his body. Perhaps his liver or lungs...impossible to know."

"So he would have been in terrible pain, wouldn't he?"

"Unbearable. Considering the pain medicine available at the time, the man must have been in agony."

"And he would have known he was dying?"

"He might not have known it was cancer, but he had to know it was something seriously wrong."

Hannah chewed her lip and stared at the screen saver of her laptop. "He killed himself to avoid dying a miserable, painful death later on. He had nothing to lose."

"He didn't, no. From what my friend said about the extent of the cancer in his bones, he was living on borrowed time."

"It's strange that no one brought that up when he was killed. At least not according to the accounts I read."

"Why would they? If he didn't have visible tumors no one would have suspected cancer back in those days. And with a note naming the killer no one had any reason to believe it was anything but murder."

"No one but Stella. She knew the note was a lie since Christopher had been with her. She was telling the truth."

"I'd say that's more than likely now. I think your theory holds up based on what we can determine from Josiah's remains. The angle of the bullet hitting the bone suggests he fired the gun himself, as does the GSR, obviously."

Hannah was silent; her mind racing as she tried to process the findings Tim had shared.

"Have you learned anything about what happened to Stella?" he asked.

"No. I haven't had a chance to look into it. I'm going to start with marriage and death records though. Census records too. I can find those things online but I'm probably going to have to go back to the Vineyard as well. Now that I've learned all this I'm anxious to get back to it."

"I can understand that. If you're not too tied up I'd still love to have that dinner sometime though."

Hannah could imagine his smile through the phone. "I'm definitely not too tied up. You pick the time and the place and I'll be there."

"Sounds good. I'll get back with you soon."

"Tim, thanks so much for what you've done for me. I can't say enough how much I appreciate it."

"You're very welcome. It's been my pleasure. I love this sort of thing, I told you that. And honestly? You've got me curious to know what happened to Stella too."

"When I find out you'll be the first to know."

"Great. I'll talk to you soon, Hannah."

"Thank you again."

Hannah put her phone back on her desk and stared out at the sidewalk below her window. She had forgotten completely about the article waiting for her attention on her laptop. She had her story now, she knew it. After putting the pieces together, it didn't take much imagination to understand what Josiah Winslow had done.

****

1884   .

Josiah slammed the door of his home and watched Stella through the window as she pulled herself up from the porch and made her way out to the street. She turned onto the road and was quickly out of sight. Josiah's lip curled up in disgust. He had no doubts about where she was headed. He knew perfectly well she would run to Menemsha and her Irish lover.

He grimaced as a fresh wave of pain washed over him. It was coming from everywhere now, and he was no longer able to say what part of his body hurt the most. It was all the same. And it was constant agony. He'd taken all the laudanum he could take and still function, and it did nothing. He knew he was past the point of anything helping him.

He slowly stumbled to his office and sat down in his chair. At least that brought a little relief to his legs. The pain of his weight when he was standing had become unbearable. Josiah pulled a bottle of laudanum out of his desk drawer and swallowed all of the contents. It may not help much, but at least it was something.

The only time he'd felt even a second of relief from the pain was when he'd been lashing out at Stella. He supposed the adrenalin had simply taken over. That, and his rage had eclipsed even the pain that crippled him.

After all he had been through in his life, working his way from a poor farm boy to an educated and respected island doctor, he never could have imagined it would all come to this in the end. His wife flaunting her infidelity and her young lover in front of his peers and neighbors. As if the agony of his illness wasn't enough, now he would be remembered as a cuckold and a pathetic fool.

Josiah thought of Lillian and ached again for the woman he had always loved. She would never have treated him this way. He felt a moment of shame as he realized she would never have approved of his beating of Stella, either. He knew he had gone too far. But the hussy had brought out the worst in him. If only she'd shown him the minimum of respect, she could have saved herself from that beating. And not just the beating. She could have saved herself what was to come, too. She'd made her bed and Josiah felt no shame about making her lie in it.

He pulled a handkerchief from his pocket and wiped his brow. The laudanum had started to take the sharp edges off the pain for now but he knew he didn't have much time to act before it took over again. He'd gone through that for the last time.

Josiah was dying, a fact he'd known for weeks now. He didn't know exactly what had taken over his body, but it was crystal clear that it had been invaded by a disease that had no intention of letting him go. But Josiah also knew he wasn't helpless against the invader. He still had one way of maintaining control and refusing to allow the pain to have its way with him any longer. He knew his death was inevitable. But he could still decide when that death would come.

And he could decide whether or not his unfaithful hussy of a wife could live out the rest of her days with her lover. Perhaps if he'd been a more forgiving man, Josiah would have allowed Stella to find the happiness he knew she'd never found with him, nor he with her. But he wasn't a forgiving man. And when it came to Stella, any care he had once felt for the girl had turned to a burning hatred.

He'd spent years trying to swallow the resentment he felt towards her when she couldn't even bear him a son to carry on his name. Had that been so much to ask? A son to mentor and teach his trade, so that one day the boy could take over his medical practice? He hadn't thought so. And now he'd be damned if he'd give Stella the opportunity to try to have another man's child.

He could have killed her when he was beating her and, for a brief moment, he had thought that was what he was going to do. But he had regained his senses in time. Dying would have been too easy for her. He wanted her to suffer, just as he had suffered through the agonizing torment of his illness and slow death.

Josiah knew that it wouldn't be long before his wife was in the arms of her lover. She would imagine herself running away with him and leaving Josiah behind to be whispered about and pitied. She had no idea.

He opened his desk drawer and removed his gun, an 1875 Schofield revolver. He set it on the desk in front of him and grabbed his prescription notepad. He dipped his pen in the inkwell next to the pad and held it with his left hand. He wanted his writing to look as messy as possible and, as a natural right-hander, this would do the trick.

Josiah smiled grimly as he grasped the pen and wrote out "Christopher Casey shot me" in a shaky, barely legible penmanship. The writing looked like it had been done by a man in terrible distress and pain. Just as he wanted it to look. He pulled the note off the pad, purposely tearing the edge of the paper, and let it fall to the floor next to his desk.

He knew Zebediah Johnson and Jon Coffin would be at his door early tomorrow morning to purchase medicines from him. Those two fools could be counted on to be here every Wednesday, like clockwork. He imagined the two of them knocking on his door and calling out for both him and Stella. When no one answered, they'd fret a bit about whether to go inside, finally deciding it would be for the best. Josiah only wished he could be here to see the events that would unfold after the two idiots found his dead body.

"Oh, Stella," he whispered. "I did warn you I wasn't finished, didn't I?"

Josiah could already feel the laudanum wearing off and he had no intention of letting another wave of pain overtake him. He stood up from his chair and picked up his revolver.

"I'll be with you soon, Lillian," he said, as he brought the gun up to his chest.

Josiah pressed the barrel of the revolver under his ribcage and angled it towards his heart. He glanced down at the note next to his feet and smiled as he curled his finger around the trigger.

Josiah pulled the trigger and fired the gun, sending the bullet blasting into his chest. He lost consciousness as he toppled onto the floor. His blood sprayed across the note beside him.

****

2013

*H*annah had never been so grateful for the popularity of genealogy research online. In the past, she would have spent hours going to county clerks' offices and state libraries for vital records and census information from the 19th century. Now all she had to do was sign up for one of the big genealogy sites and more information than she would have believed possible was suddenly at her fingertips from the comfort of her own bedroom.

After realizing that she knew nothing about Stella before she became the wife of Josiah Winslow, Hannah set out to find marriage records from the time. Considering how young Stella looked in the 1884 photo, Hannah doubted she had been married to Josiah long before the photo was taken. She browsed through the Dukes County, Massachusetts marriage licenses from a few years before the time of the photo, finally stumbling on a Winslow license. Josiah Winslow had married Stella Hammett in 1879 on the Hammett family farm in Chilmark.

Hannah stopped browsing and leaned back in her chair. The Hammett farm. Could this be the same land where the Hammett House resided today? She knew land surrounding the bed & breakfast had once been farmland, and that the house itself was a restored farm house. Could this be the same Stella Hammett?

Hannah knew that Hammett was a common surname historically on Martha's Vineyard. But how many Hammett families lived on farms in Chilmark? She couldn't believe it was a coincidence. And she felt a shiver down her spine as she remembered how she had decided to stay at the Hammett House out of the blue while making her trip plans. Had Stella been leading her then, too? It seemed likely now. No wonder Stella had been able to leave the newspaper articles in her room. Had the room she slept in once been Stella's?

Switching to birth records and census documents, Hannah tried to find information on the Hammett family. After a considerable amount of digging, she came upon a birth certificate for Stella Anne Hammett, daughter of Charles and Alma. She couldn't find any other children for the couple, and wondered if Stella had been an only child. Digging through more records, she found death certificates for both Charles and Alma. Both had died of consumption in 1879, no more than a few months before Stella married Josiah.

Hannah thought of the ghost she had seen on the webcam and tried to imagine what it would have been like for a 15 year old girl to lose her parents and have no choice but to marry a man old enough to be her father. Clearly Josiah had taken ownership of the farm upon marrying the Hammett's only daughter.

Once again, Hannah felt an inexorable tie to Stella. She knew exactly how it felt to lose both parents at the same time. She was just glad she had been old enough to take care of herself when her loss had happened. And that she lived in an era where an independent woman was not a rarity and a woman living on her own was considered acceptable. Stella had had no such luxury.

Hannah returned to the marriage records and tried to find a later marriage for Stella. She would have been so young when Josiah died and Christopher was murdered, barely more than 20, and it would have been understandable if she had married again. But Hannah could find no trace of Stella Winslow at all in later records.

She got up from her chair and paced the room, wishing she could simply ask Stella's ghost what had happened to her next. She sat back down and brought up the webcam again, finding a crowd of tourists just getting off a tour bus and climbing the steps to the overlook. It was a sunny summer day on the island now, and the Aquinnah shops and restaurants would be counting on the tourists to keep their businesses successful. Hannah couldn't imagine the ghost returning to the overlook in the midst of a crowd like this. And she knew she couldn't ask for any answers from Stella even if she could see her.

It dawned on Hannah that perhaps the answer had been under her nose twice already, but she simply hadn't realized it. She knew that the owner of the Hammett House B&B had lived on the island for her entire life before purchasing and restoring the old house. Hannah checked her memory for the articles she had read about the B&B before staying there, and remembered the owner had been a lover of history which was one of the things that had drawn her to the old house. Perhaps Grace Pease knew about the original owners of the property. Hannah had never thought to ask her.

There was no time like the present to change that. Hannah grabbed her phone from her desk and brought up the number for the Hammett House. Grace Pease answered the call after just two rings.

"Hammett House. How can I help you?"

"Ms. Pease? This is Hannah Forrester." Hannah knew Pease would remember her, as it was unlikely that she had guests make two trips to her place in such a short time frame.

"Ms. Forrester, hello. How are you today?"

"Fine, thank you. Ms. Pease, I wonder if I could ask you a few questions."

Hannah briefly explained her purpose to the B&B caretaker, telling her about her plans for a book and the research she had been doing on the wreck of *The City of Columbus*, which had led her to Stella Hammett.

"Do you know anything about the original owners of the house, the Hammett family?"

"I know that Charles Hammett and his wife Alma died of consumption, and the farm was passed on to their only daughter and her husband, the town doctor."

"That would be Stella. Their daughter, I mean."

"Right."

"What happened to the farm after that?"

"It gets fuzzy then. Apparently the doctor sold off most of the land to a neighbor and the house fell to the town when he was murdered some years later. Have you read about that murder in your research? It was quite sensational. Murder was nearly unheard of on the island in those days."

"I have read about it, yes. But why did the town take ownership of the house? Stella Hammett was alive when her husband was murdered."

"Yes, but apparently she disappeared not long after the murder. The records on what happened to her aren't clear. All I know is the town of Chilmark owned the house and ultimately sold it to another family in the late 1880s."

Hannah sighed. Another dead end.

"I'm sorry I can't be of more help, Ms. Forrester."

"Oh, no, you have been helpful, thank you. Tell me, do you happen to know when the property was turned over to the town?"

"Not exactly. I only know it was shortly after the doctor was murdered."

"Thank you again, Ms. Pease. I appreciate your taking the time to talk to me."

"My pleasure. I hope we see you again here soon."

"You just might," Hannah said, ending the call.

Hannah set her phone back on her desk and chewed her lip as she pondered the latest bit of information. What on earth had happened to Stella after Christopher's murder? Had she ever even returned to her house?

She browsed through more records online but knew her research wasn't going to get anywhere. The only way she might find out what happened to Stella was by reviewing the old newspapers. If there had been a missing person's case, the papers might have covered it. Remembering the Boston Globe reporter Chesham, Hannah wondered if he had continued to follow up on island events after his disgust over the resolution to Christopher's murder.

There was really only one way to find out, and Hannah knew it wasn't online. She'd have to return to the old newspaper reels. But she might not have to return to the island itself. Now that she knew who and what she was looking for, she could probably find the information she needed much closer to home. Hannah picked up her phone and grabbed her purse from the coat rack near her closet. She didn't have to go far to find old New England newspapers. She left her apartment and headed for Cambridge and the Harvard University library.

****

It felt strange to be back in the Harvard library where Hannah had spent so much time as an undergraduate. While she was only 32, she now felt ancient as she looked around at the fresh-faced students sitting at the nearby tables. Had her face ever looked that young?

She forced herself to cut her pity party short and focus on the newspapers in front of her. She searched the Boston Globe for any further articles on Stella and the Christopher Casey murder, but found nothing from Arthur Chesham. He had apparently moved on and stuck to writing about the mainland.

Hannah returned to the newspaper desk and asked for the films of the Vineyard Gazette from the latter half of 1884. She took the bundle of microfilm and wearily returned to the reader. She was definitely going to need reading glasses before this was all over. She felt sure overexposure to microfilm could bring on blindness to anyone unfortunate enough to have to read it regularly.

She browsed through the Gazette articles, yawning as she skimmed stories on church dinners, sewing circles, and the abundance of strawberries available that year at the Tisbury Farmer's Market. Just when she was about to give up, she came upon a small article about Stella and another name she recognized, the lighthouse keeper William Mayhew. Hannah remembered that the keeper and his wife had tried to come to Christopher's aid and were seemingly the only people on the island who believed in his innocence.

Hannah rubbed her eyes and sat back to read. She knew she had finally found what she was looking for.

****

1884

Stella rolled over in the bed and stared with bloodshot eyes at the sun shining through the window. She squinted in the light and pulled the thin blanket over her face to cover her eyes. She had no interest in seeing the dawn of another hopeless day.

She loved being in the bed, anyway. It was the same bed Christopher had lain in while she had cared for him after the shipwreck. Stella felt as if she was somehow still close to him here in this bed. While she knew Mrs. Mayhew had long since washed the bed linens, she still imagined they carried the faint scent of Christopher in their folds.

It was ironic to realize now that Christopher would have been much better off if the sea had simply swept him away from the wreck of *The City of Columbus* and he hadn't survived to find himself on the shores of Martha's Vineyard. It would have been far kinder to the man in the end had he never come to this place. Or more pointedly, never come to her. She had cared for him and dressed his wounds only to bring him right to his death, as surely as if she had held the gun that killed him herself.

Stella rolled over again and faced the wall. She didn't want to think of all that anymore. She couldn't bear to see the torches burning in the night sky or to hear the screams and the deafening blast of the rifle. She longed to banish the stench of blood and gunpowder from her nose.

Mr. and Mrs. Mayhew had been kind enough to allow her to stay with them after the rest of the island had turned on her and branded her a whore and a strumpet. She still flinched when she recalled the looks her neighbors had given her when she had told the truth about Christopher's murder and the vigilante actions of Zebediah Johnson and his gang of monsters. If Mr. and Mrs. Mayhew hadn't intervened, she had no doubt that she would have been sent to the mainland and locked up in a psychiatric asylum after she had screamed and collapsed on the courtroom floor in hysteria when Johnson had been set free.

She was grateful to the Mayhews, but she knew she couldn't stay in their home much longer. She couldn't abuse their hospitality and kindness, although she knew they would never ask her to leave. Regardless, she knew it was time for her to go.

Stella finally sat up and forced her legs off the bed and her feet onto the floor. She stood up and shuffled forward, feeling as if each small step sapped her energy and threatened to pull her down into a heap on the floor. She finally made it to the bureau across from the bed and dressed in her white cotton dress. She tied her bonnet around her neck and let it hang down her back. She would want to put that on later when she was out in the wind, but there was no need to fasten it around her head now. Feeling a chill, she pulled her navy blue cape across her shoulders before heading out of the room and towards the Mayhew kitchen.

Stella hoped to find the kitchen empty when she entered, but instead saw Mrs. Mayhew standing at her stove. She was stirring something in a pot, with her back to Stella. She turned around when she heard Stella's footsteps behind her.

"Good morning, Stella. Would you like some oatmeal?"

Stella felt sure that she would vomit if she ate anything, but she couldn't let that show. "That would be lovely, Mrs. Mayhew. Thank you."

"Take a seat, child. I'll get you some coffee too. You can feel autumn coming in the air today."

"Where's Mr. Mayhew this morning?"

"He's up in the lighthouse cleaning the windows. Got an early start today."

Mrs. Mayhew brought a cup of steaming hot coffee and a bowl of oatmeal to the table and set both down in front of Stella. She took the seat next to her and sat down herself.

"Please eat something, Stella."

Stella nodded. "Of course. I can't resist your cooking, you know that."

Mrs. Mayhew knew the girl was lying. She had done nothing but push food around on her plate or in her bowl for days now. Her cheeks were gaunt and the bones of her arms were turning into sticks.

"I'm worried about you, you know that. You've lost too much weight."

Stella couldn't help but think that she'd lost much more than weight. She'd actually lost everything. And everyone. But she managed a feeble smile.

"I don't want to worry you," she said. "I'm fine, I promise."

Stella took comfort in the fact that she wasn't actually lying to the only woman who had shown her kindness since this whole ordeal had begun. She would be fine soon. She was going to make sure of that.

"Have you thought about what you're going to do next, child? Not that you're not welcome here, of course. You know you have a home here with us as long as you need it."

"I know that, and I'm grateful. But I'll be moving on soon. I don't want to be a burden to you."

"You're not a burden to us. Not at all."

"Not yet, maybe. But I dare say that will change if I wear out my welcome."

"That won't happen."

Stella took a spoon full of oatmeal and forced herself to swallow it. No, it won't, she thought.

Mrs. Mayhew got up from the table. "I've got some laundry to do so I'll get to it. There's more oatmeal in the pot. Eat as much as you want, please."

"I will, thank you." Stella glanced out the window at the sun shining over the water. "It looks like a beautiful day. I think I'll take a little walk and get some fresh air after I finish."

"That sounds like a good idea. Get outside and get some color back into those cheeks of yours. I dare say you should take Grover and go for a ride. It would be good for both of you."

Stella watched Mrs. Mayhew leave the room and felt tears stinging the corner of her eyes. She knew what she had planned would upset both the woman and her husband. But it had to be done. And maybe they would never even know exactly what happened.

She let out a breath and pushed the uneaten oatmeal away from her. Standing up from the table, she took both the bowl and her cup and returned them to the sink. She cleaned both and put the wet dishes in the drying tray on the sink. Taking a look around the kitchen, she pulled her cape around her shoulders and walked outside to the cliffs.

The wind hit her immediately and blew her hair back from her face. She pulled up her bonnet, capturing her hair inside it, and tied the strings under her chin. Pulling her cape more tightly around her shoulders, Stella walked to the path that led down to the shore. She tried not to look at the ground as she got to the path, as she knew she would see Christopher's blood spilled all over the sand in spite of the fact that it had been washed away by a torrential rainstorm on the day after the murder. For Stella, it was always there.

She stopped at the path and glanced back towards the lighthouse, where she could see Mr. Mayhew on a ladder scrubbing the glass of the windows. He wasn't looking in her direction, and she doubted he would have noticed her either way. She blew a kiss towards the house and murmured a special goodbye to Grover. With that, she quickly turned and headed down the path.

Her feet sunk into the sand of the beach and she could feel drops of water from the high waves splashing her face. She walked down to the shoreline and let the waves hit her, standing perfectly still as they crashed around her and drenched her up to her waist. Stella shivered from the freezing cold water but continued to stand still and stare out at the horizon.

She pictured Christopher hanging on to the rigging of *The City of Columbus* as it sunk into the water directly in front of where she was now standing. He had told her how he had looked up at the lighthouse beacon and counted the seconds each time it rotated and appeared again. The beam shining through the darkness had been the one thing that had given him hope through that long and dark January night. He had held on to that beacon.

For Stella, there was no beacon. Nothing to give her any hope. She knew that was gone, just as her home, her family, her sheep, her dog, and her Christopher were all gone. There was nothing left for her.

Stella let out a deep and cleansing breath and moved forward on the sand, ignoring the icy water that now splashed up to her shoulders. She wondered if Christopher was waiting for her out in the sea where his dead body had been so ruthlessly tossed. She thought of the day she had taught him how to shear sheep and smiled as she remembered the sound of his laughter when the sheep knocked him to the ground. Perhaps his spirit would be out beyond the waves, there to welcome her to another world, and she would hear that laughter again. The promise and possibility gave her renewed strength to keep going as wave after wave crashed over her and drenched her face and bonnet. The strength of each successive wave threatened to knock her down.

Stella put her arms out to steady herself. She kept walking.

****

2013

"So she killed herself?" Tim asked.

"Yes. She walked into the ocean at Aquinnah and drowned." Hannah shook her head as she recalled what she had read. "The lighthouse keeper was washing the windows of the lighthouse when she did it. He saw her walking forward into the waves. He ran down the stairs and out of the lighthouse, yelling for her to stop, but by the time he got down to the beach she was long gone. He saw the final wave knock her over and sweep her away as he was running down the trail that led to the beach."

"I guess if he hadn't seen her, no one ever would have known what happened to her."

"No, I don't think they would have. Her body was never found. And honestly, there wasn't much coverage of what happened anyway. I think the islanders wanted to put the whole scandal behind them."

Tim sat back in his chair at the Skylight restaurant and frowned. "What a terrible story."

"Isn't it? And to think she was only 20 years old. Such a waste."

"I guess she must have felt like she didn't have anyone left. Or anything."

"Which was true, really. Except for the lighthouse keeper and his wife, it seems like the whole island turned on her. And that was the only home she'd ever known."

"Shitty world sometimes, isn't it?"

Hannah nodded. "I guess it always has been." She took a sip of her wine and leaned back in her chair. "As bad as I feel for Stella though, Christopher is the one I feel most sorry for. Talk about getting screwed left and right."

"Yeah, if he came here in the first place, his life in Ireland couldn't have been anything to write home about. Then he finds himself in a shipwreck. Only to survive and end up murdered for a crime he didn't commit." Tim shook his head. "Poor guy couldn't catch a break."

"I think I feel bad too because he's so anonymous. There's a picture of Stella and Josiah, and even of the lighthouse keeper. But Christopher's a complete mystery. We don't even know what he looked like. He's just a name known for nothing but supposedly killing Josiah Winslow."

"This is a depressing topic for our first official date," Tim said.

"It is, isn't it?" Hannah said with a smile. "I'm sorry."

"Don't be. I feel like the luckiest guy in Boston being here with you in that dress."

Hannah blushed and felt her cheeks burning red. After years with Jon, she was no longer used to compliments in spite of the fact that other men had appreciated her looks for as long as she could remember.

"Well, if you really want to feel special," she said, "I can tell you that I bought the dress specifically for this occasion."

"See, that proves it. I knew I was a lucky man."

Hannah laughed and twirled a strand of linguine around her fork. She had always wanted to try the Skylight, one of the few five star restaurants in Boston, but Jon had always thought it was a waste of money. When Tim suggested it, she couldn't resist taking him up on it. And she wasn't lying; she had bought a new dress for their dinner.

While she hated to admit it, she had been aghast when she'd searched her closet for a decent dress to wear to dinner. She had been away from office work long enough that she had become lazy with her wardrobe. While she loved working at home and wearing sweats and t-shirts, it hadn't been the best thing for her choices in clothing. She actually couldn't remember the last time she'd bought a good dress.

Hannah had found a black lace sheath dress with short sleeves and a jewel neck. A belt emphasized her curves and long waist. Paired with platform black heels, the dress was both flattering and sophisticated. She tied her hair into a flipped bun and finished the look with a pair of sterling silver drop earrings with black rectangles. Hannah knew she looked good, and it felt great to be able to say that.

Her date's look had made her smile even more. She had only seen Tim in jeans and a casual shirt, so when he had shown up at her door wearing a wine-colored Versace blazer and black dress pants, his stunning good looks had caught her by surprise.

Now as she smiled at him across the table, she felt like the luckiest woman in the room as well.

A familiar figure caught Hannah's attention out of the corner of her eye, interrupting the good mood of the dinner. She turned to see Jon walking towards her table, hand in hand with Becky. Jon wore a grey Dolce & Gabbana suit that Hannah instantly remembered. She had innocently asked him why he had bought such an expensive suit when he hated dressing up. Now she supposed she had her answer. Becky was dressed in a silver cocktail dress that showed off her ample cleavage. Hannah felt her stomach tighten as they approached. The arrogant smirk on Jon's face was something she hadn't missed in the slightest.

"Hannah," Jon said as he and his companion came closer to the table she shared with Tim. "How are you?"

Hannah plastered a smile across her face. "I'm fine, Jon. Good to see you." She nodded towards the woman beside him. "Becky."

"Hi, Hannah."

Before Hannah had a chance to introduce him, Becky turned towards Tim, her eyes growing wide. Seeing Jon's frown, Hannah fought to keep herself from laughing. It was abundantly clear that he hadn't even noticed Tim when he was so intent on making his way towards Hannah's table.

"Oh my gosh," Becky said. "I think I know you from tv." She raised a hand to her mouth in an "I can't believe it" gesture. "History's Mysteries, right?"

Tim's face broke into the drop-dead gorgeous smile that had won him so many female fans during his brief stint on television. He stood up from his chair in gentlemanly fashion.

"Guilty as charged," he said. "I'm always so amazed to find anyone who watched the show."

"Oh, I loved it," Becky said. She extended her hand to his. "I'm Becky Sanders."

"Nice to meet you, Becky. As you already know, I'm Tim Corcoran."

Hannah stood up from her seat, trying hard not to laugh as she was sure she saw steam coming out of Jon's ears.

"Jon, let me introduce you. This is my friend Tim Corcoran. Tim, Jon Rodriguez."

The two men nodded and shook hands.

"Is there going to be another season of your show?" Becky asked, causing Jon's face to redden.

"No, I'm afraid not," Tim said. "You and Hannah here seemed to be the only two people in the country who watched it."

"Oh, that's such a shame. They always cancel the good shows." Becky's eyes hadn't left Tim's face.

Hannah lowered her gaze towards the ground and bit her lip to keep from bursting out laughing. Even in a city as huge as Boston, she knew it was inevitable she'd run into Jon eventually. She couldn't have scripted this moment any better.

"Well, we should probably get to our table," Jon said. "We're here celebrating our engagement."

Hannah's stomach lurched into her throat as she took in the words. She knew very well the comment was meant to wound and, for a second, it did. But when she looked at Jon's smirk again she realized she really didn't care. Becky was welcome to him.

"How wonderful," she said. "Congratulations to you both."

"Thank you," Jon said.

Becky had the grace to look embarrassed, and finally took her eyes off Tim.

"Don't let us keep you," Hannah said.

"Right." Jon nodded again towards Tim. "Nice to meet you, Tim. And good to see you, Hannah."

"Nice meeting you both," Tim said.

Hannah sat back down and watched as Jon and Becky faded out of sight in the crowded restaurant.

"So that's the ex?" Tim asked, bringing her attention back to her table and her own date.

"Yep, that's him. Real prize, isn't he?"

Tim chuckled. "Seemed kind of full of himself."

"You don't know the half of it."

"I know something about exes," Tim said. "That couldn't have been easy."

Hannah sighed and took a sip of wine. "You're right, it wasn't." She grinned across the table. "But it was made remarkably easier by the fact that my dear ex's fiancée only had eyes for you."

"Can you blame her?"

Hannah laughed. She met Tim's eyes across the table. "No," she said truthfully. "Actually, I can't."

Tim smiled. "You're making me blush."

"I'm just telling the truth."

Tim raised his glass and clinked it against hers. "Here's to being better off without our exes."

"Here, here," Hannah said.

"Because I can tell you in all honesty that you're better off without that guy. I'm a professional investigator, remember? I know these things."

"You investigate skeletons."

"Doesn't mean I can't see that guy's an asshole."

Hannah laughed again. "It doesn't take an investigator to see that."

She finished her wine and refilled her glass. "Listen, I don't want to talk about Jon anymore. He's a boring subject."

"That he is. Let's go back to your ghost."

"Okay. What about her?"

"Are you going to write the book? Now that you know how she ended up, I mean."

Hannah pondered the question as she took another sip of wine. "I've thought about that, and thought maybe I'd let it go. But I finally decided that wouldn't be right. I am still going to write it. I think she came to me because she wanted her story to be told."

"I think so too," Tim said. "I'm glad you're writing it."

"I owe it to her, really."

"Why?"

Hannah shrugged. "It's kind of weird, but I feel like she saved my life." She let out a breath. "I feel guilty saying that considering what happened to her, but it's the truth."

"Were you in that bad of a situation when you first learned about her?" Tim said, suddenly looking alarmed.

"No, no," Hannah said. "I guess saying she saved my life is too dramatic. It's more accurate to say she helped me get moving again. I'd been stuck in neutral ever since I lost my parents."

"Maybe she knew that," Tim said.

"Maybe so. That would be nice."

Tim raised his glass again. "To Stella, then."

Hannah smiled and clinked his glass. "To Stella. And to Christopher Casey, too. I think he's another big reason I want to write the book. I think it's time someone cleared the poor guy's name."

She grimaced as she somehow heard the sound of Jon's laughter over the noise of the crowded restaurant.

"You want to get out of here?" Tim asked.

"Yeah. I really do."

"Great. I do too." He signaled towards their waiter. "I'll take care of it."

Tim quickly paid the bill and smiled across the table at Hannah.

"Let's get going," he said.

Hannah returned his smile and stood up from her chair. She ignored the sound of Jon's laughter as she and Tim left the restaurant hand in hand.

***

Hannah knew that when it came to getting her book published, she was lucky to already be working as a writer and to have colleagues in the business. And so it was that, while she didn't have her book on Stella and Christopher completed yet, she was able to make an appointment to meet with Stephanie Morgan, the owner of an independent press that focused on stories of New England. Simply called New England Press, Hannah had learned of the publisher when she worked with Morgan on an article about the history of the towns of Cape Cod for a regional magazine. Both women shared a love of history and of New England, and Hannah had gambled that Morgan would be interested in her book proposal and decided to contact her.

Now as they had breakfast together in the Red Sox Café, Hannah knew that her gamble had paid off. As she had given Morgan an outline of her project, including as many details as she could, she had seen her colleague's interest grow with each word she said.

"Oh my God, I love it," Stephanie said as she took a sip of her Earl Grey tea and bit into her buttered English muffin. "How did you find out about this?"

As she always did, Hannah kept the detail of Stella's ghost out of her explanation. "I told you, I came upon the story of the wreck of *The City of Columbus* when I was researching the Gay Head light for my book on lighthouses. I was on the island looking at the historical society exhibit about the wreck and one thing led to another."

Stephanie looked at the muffin in her hand as she listened to Hannah's account. "God I love the muffins they serve here. What makes them so much different?"

"I don't know, but I love them too."

Stephanie took another bite and smiled. "I can't get enough of them. And I can't get enough of this story of yours either."

"So does that mean you're interested?"

"Of course I'm interested. What else could I love it and I can't get enough of it mean?

Hannah laughed. "I just want to make sure. I know how you publishers can be."

"When do you think you can have the manuscript written?"

"Probably within seven or eight months. I already have most of the story in my head anyway. But I didn't take any notes while I was researching the story on the Vineyard so I'm going to need to go through my sources again and get all my documentation cited and in order. Plus we need to figure out the logistics of having Tim involved."

"Tim Corcoran." Stephanie laughed as she took another bite of her muffin. "I still can't believe you have him on board. I loved him on History's Mysteries."

"You and every other woman who watched it. Too bad there weren't more of us."

"I'll get a contract set up with him once you get the book finished, we should have some funds to pay him as a consultant."

Hannah finished her coffee and put down her mug. "What's the next step?"

"I'd love to give you a contract with an advance, but we don't have the money for advances anymore, I'm sorry."

"It's okay, I didn't expect one. I know how the publishing industry is now."

"I can give you a contract for future publication though. I really want this for New England Press. I think it's perfect."

"You're not worried the story might be too sad?"

"Are you kidding? Some of the most famous stories in the world are tragedies. Romeo & Juliet ring any bells?"

"I know, but these were real people."

"That makes it even more important to tell their story. And I think readers will be totally drawn into it. Doomed young lovers, an immigrant falsely accused of a crime he didn't commit... I think people will like the idea of his name being cleared after all these years. Americans love to see a wrong righted or justice served. And we know how many Americans count the Irish immigrants among their ancestors. They'd love the idea of the truth about Mr. Casey finally being told."

Stephanie finished her tea and took a last bite of her English muffin.

"Hannah, listen to me," she said. "I think this has all the ingredients of a big seller. And if I'm being honest, I think it's a chance to get New England Press on the map."

Hannah blushed. "I'm thrilled you have so much confidence in my story. I hope it's justified."

"It will be. Listen, I'll send you a copy of the contract so you can go over it. But please, don't waste any time getting started on the book."

"I definitely won't. I've been dying to write it anyway."

Stephanie reached across the table and extended her hand to Hannah. "We've got a deal then, partner. I can't wait to read that book."

****

Nine Months Later

Hannah gently moved Tim's arm from across her shoulders and slipped out of bed, trying her best not to wake him. She knew she should be sleeping herself, but she couldn't stop thinking about her book. After countless rewrites, she had finished the manuscript and was now waiting on the final proof from Stephanie so she could review her work before it officially went to press.

Hannah put on her terry-cloth robe, took her laptop from her desk, and walked to the living room, where she could work without disturbing Tim's sleep. She plopped down on Tim's camel-colored leather sofa and grabbed her lap desk from the coffee table. Covering herself with Tim's beloved Cincinnati Reds throw, she stretched out her legs on the sofa, put the desk and laptop on her lap, and booted up her computer. Tim's dogs Lucy and Harris got up from their respective beds and came to greet her. She petted their heads and encouraged both of them to jump up on the couch with her. They could all be bad together while Daddy was sleeping.

With Harris' head on her lapand Lucy curled up at her feet, Hannah held her breath while she logged in to her email and waited for new messages to load. To her disappointment, she had nothing new but a spam message inviting her to try a new diet supplement and lose 50 pounds. Hannah knew she shouldn't have had her hopes up that there would be a message waiting for her from Stephanie, as she had just checked her mail a few hours ago before she and Tim had gone to bed. But she knew Stephanie liked to work late, and she had hoped that perhaps she would have surprised her with a response.

Feeling restless, Hannah still didn't want to go back to bed as she knew she'd never be able to fall asleep. She decided to work out some details for her upcoming trip to the Vineyard with Tim. Now that her work was completed, she wanted to bring Tim to the island for a reason beyond digging up an old skeleton. She wanted to show him her grandparents' cottage and all of her favorite spots. As her mother had done with her father, Hannah wanted to show Tim the island she loved.

She brought up the Martha's Vineyard website in her browser and couldn't resist clicking on the Aquinnah webcams. She looked at the camera overlooking the beach first, although she didn't really expect to see anything since it was nearly midnight. To her surprise, the full moon shone brightly over the water and combined with the stars in the clear sky to give her enough light to see the waves lapping against the shore.

As always, Hannah was struck by the timelessness of the ocean. She felt a stab in her heart as she looked at the same waves that Stella had walked into to her death. The same waves that Christopher's body had been so carelessly thrown into. And the same water where Christopher had clung to the rigging of the sinking *City of Columbus*. She wondered how many other countless lives had come and gone in the years since these waves had first started licking the shores of the island.

Hannah switched to the lighthouse camera and smiled at the bright beacon that never failed to shine at the camera every ten seconds. The bushes around the steps that blew in the night breeze were the only signs of life on the camera.

Hannah hadn't expected anything different, but she realized as she clicked on the camera's page that she was hoping to see Stella return to the overlook steps and make contact with her. She wanted to see her again, even if it was only one more time. She wanted to let her know that her story was going to be told.

But as Hannah stared at the landscape surrounding the lighthouse, no one appeared. Hannah let out a breath and nuzzled the ears of the dog in her lap. She couldn't explain it, but she somehow knew that she had seen Stella for the last time. The tiny woman in the long white dress and dark blue cape wasn't going to appear to her again. Hannah wished she'd been able to say goodbye.

Hannah stared at the scene on the webcam until she nearly fell into a trance. She jumped when she heard the beeping sound that indicated she had a new message in her email inbox.

She looked at Harris, who had also jumped at the sound and now stared at her expectantly.

"Do you think it's from Stephanie, Harris?" she asked.

The dog licked her hand in response.

"I think it is too," she said, giving his ears another scratch.

Hannah held her breath as she closed out of the webcam and brought up her email. She nearly squealed in excitement when she saw the new message was indeed from Stephanie. Obviously the publisher's habit of working late had not changed.

She opened the email and had to suppress a squeal again when she saw the final proof of her manuscript attached to a quick note from Stephanie.

"It's the manuscript, Harris," she whispered. "I think it's finished."

Hannah knew she'd never go to sleep now. She downloaded the attachment to her laptop, and her face broke into a smile as she opened the document and saw the title page.

"The Ghosts of Aquinnah: The Story of Stella Winslow and Christopher Casey"

216

Hannah settled back into the couch cushions and began to read.

****

Stella stood in the trees and watched a woman and a young boy sitting at the picnic table across the driveway from the stairs leading up to the overlook. The woman looked to be about thirty, and she wore her long blonde hair piled in a bun on top of her head. The boy, who was clearly her son, was no more than five and had blonde hair and blue eyes to match his mother's. The woman had bought cookies and hot chocolate for herself and the child as they had watched the sun set over the water. Now, she helped her son button up his jacket against the night breeze as he finished his drink.

The boy downed the last of his hot chocolate and hopped off the bench to throw his Styrofoam cup into a nearby wastebasket. His mother rose from the bench as well and grabbed the child's hand in her own. Stella could hear the boy laughing at something his mother had said to him. The woman turned towards the ocean as if to take one last look at the waves breaking against the shoreline, and then hurried to her waiting car with her son skipping along beside her. The woman turned on her car and backed out of her parking space, stopping one last time to look down at the sea below.

Stella watched the lights of the car disappear as the woman and her child drove around the circular parking lot and headed back towards Chilmark and the rest of the island. As the lights faded away, Stella came out from among the trees. There were no more tourists left tonight. Stella was alone. She walked over to the table and ran her hand along where the boy and his mother had been seated. Not for the first time, she wondered what if would have been like to be a mother herself.

Pulling her blue cape closer to her chest, Stella scolded herself for such nonsensical thinking after all this time. Her inability to be a mother while she had lived was the last thing she needed to worry about now. And it was such a long time ago, anyway.

Stella didn't need to worry about motherhood or any such issues now. She finally had what she wanted. When she'd stood at the shoreline and watched the waves before walking into the sea to her death, she'd promised Christopher that somehow, someday, she would clear his name. She'd find a way to make sure that the world knew that the kind and gentle young man she'd known and loved was not a murderer. Now, after all these years, she could finally say she'd kept her promise.

Stella couldn't say for sure what had drawn her to the lonely woman who looked at the webcam so frequently. She'd watched Hannah Forrester for quite some time before making the decision to reveal herself to her. Stella had felt pity for the woman, and a connection to her that somehow crossed time. To Stella, the pretty woman who stared at the webcam seemed lost and alone in spite of the fact that she lived in a city overflowing with people. The very city Stella had longed to visit while she lived.

The more Stella watched Hannah Forrester, the more she felt that the woman was hoping to find someone or something she'd lost each time she stared at the cliffs and the sea below them. Stella knew all about that hope.

She'd taken a chance and connected with the woman, letting her understand who and what she was. And leading her in the only way she knew how to the story of the young man she'd loved and failed so horribly. To Stella's immense relief, her decision had paid off.

Now, Stella's debt was paid and there was no longer any need for her to remain on this island, trapped somewhere between the living and the dead. Perhaps now she could finally see her Christopher again. She turned and glanced back at the lighthouse, remembering the day she had watched Mr. Mayhew clean the windows before she had walked to her death. So many years had passed between that day and now. So many waves had crashed into the shoreline, dragging sand and shells back with them into the sea.

Stella was tired now, and ready to be done. She stared out at the ocean and listened to the lapping of the waves, wondering once again whether Christopher was somewhere out there, waiting for her. She hoped now she'd have a chance to find out.

Stella pulled her cape tightly to her and walked towards the cliffs and the sea. As the lighthouse beacon rotated and shone its red light over the cliffs, Stella disappeared into the mist.

The rotating light shone white. By the time the red light flashed again, the cliffs were empty. No one was there.